Carole Anne Hyde is seventy six and she has been writing love stories since 2009. Over the years, she never stopped and it became her hobby. Carole has three children, David, Jenny and Stephen, with 18 grandchildren and great grandchildren. Her husband is Fred who she married in 1967. Carole was born in Deptford in 1946 and moved to the East End of London when she was six. She has a sister Denise, who is ten years younger than her.

I would like to dedicate this book to my aunt Doris, who is now 95 years old as of the 1st of December. Since she was young, she has been an avid romance reader, and she got me hooked on reading the same books. She challenged me to write a story about a girl named September, and I did. She loved it, and that was in 2009. Doris is the reason I'm still writing stories today. When I next visit her in the nursing home she has been in since she turned 90, she will be even more excited than I am. And of course, I'm going to say, "I told you so."

To everyone at the Austin Macauley Publishing Company who decided to publish my story *The Infinity Pool*, I am still in shock.

Carole Hyde

THE INFINITY POOL

AUSTIN MACAULEY PUBLISHERS™

LONDON • CAMBRIDGE • NEW YORK • SHARJAH

A CIP catalogue record for this title is available from the British Library.

ISBN 9781398495227 (Paperback)
ISBN 9781398495234 (ePub e-book)

www.austinmacauley.com

First Published 2023
Austin Macauley Publishers Ltd®
1 Canada Square
Canary Wharf
London
E14 5AA

20230905

Lia was on her way home from work; she is twenty-six and works for Grossman and Partner, a designer consultants company. Leaving university, Lia Westlake went for an interview with the directors Tony Grossman and his partner Mark James and they love the fact Lia Westlake studied modern design and techniques; they needed fresh ideas and she suited them.

Lia was in the middle of finishing the designs for a block of luxury apartments in the Southbank. There are six and a penthouse in which the builders had incorporated a veranda on the first floor for Lia, a penthouse with a difference; it had two floors. Lia parked up and walked into the house, and Nancy was busy with a tray of drinks.

"They are waiting for you, Lia, your mum has been entertaining them."

"Who, Nancy, male or female?"

"Definitely the male one is very good looking, the other I would call distinguished." She smiled, took her coat off and looked in the mirror, her hair was fine, and she walked in.

"There you are, Lia, had a good day?"

"Yes, thank you, Mum, we have guests."

"Yes, let me introduce you."

"Gentlemen, my daughter Lia." The youngest stood up and kissed her hand; the eldest smiled at her.

7

"So what can I do for you, gentlemen? I assume it's me you were waiting to see. Nancy tells me you have been here over an hour."

"Lia, these gentlemen are solicitors and you have apparently been included in the will of an Italian gentleman."

"Miss Westlake, Russo Valentino died some three months ago, you were included in his will." Lia sat down, tears began to fall and her mum came running over.

"Darling, are you okay?" She shook her head, got up and left the room.

"Gentlemen, I have no idea who this man was and the reason my daughter is crying, but I can assure you that now is not the time to pursue whatever you came for; give me a few days and I will phone you." They left and Donna went to find her daughter who was in the kitchen. Lia was sitting with Nancy; she had a tissue and was wiping her eyes. Donna came and sat down.

"I'm sorry I had no idea who this man was who died, you apparently did, Lia, tell me who was he?"

Lia looked up. Donna could see it was causing her to cry more.

"You won't remember, but when I first went to work for Mark and Tony, there was a request for an infinity pool, they gave it to me to sort of try my hand at designing one. The infinity pool was for a villa in Florence, Italy and I set to work doing just that, and the man who wanted the pool was Russo Valentino; he was so nice, we spoke often and the design I sent him he went with and I was there if he needed to go through the design with me. Although I never went to Italy, we worked very closely together. After designing it on the hillside part of the garden, the company installed it and it went perfectly. I promised to visit but never did and now I feel guilty. Mum, he was so nice on the phone."

"Darling, you designed him a pool and it was built to the experts specifications, but you can't visit everyone, can you? Besides, he lived in Italy."

"Exactly what did those two men want, Mum?"

"Darling, they would not tell me, they wanted to speak to you, but it must have been important as they were here an hour; they left their phone number; they are solicitors. Now we need to get some food into you, Lia, worry about the solicitors tomorrow."

The next day, Lia left for work a little earlier than usual. She drove to the solicitors 'office; she had googled them, John and James Simons, they were son and father and very much your upper class solicitors. She walked into reception and told the woman on the desk she needed to speak to either John or James Simons as it was urgent. Both were not in the office and it was 9.30, so she left and went to work. Whatever it was they wanted it would have to wait, she was too busy with this renovation. Lia got to the building, the construction was almost finished; she donned a hard hat and walked in. The workers took no notice of her in jeans, boots and her jacket, she looked like one of them. She walked up the stairs and into the office which was her own until the job was finished…Cathy made her tea.

"You're late, not like you. Everything okay, Lia?"

"Yes, I went to see a solicitor or solicitors this morning, but at 9.30, they were not in so I left."

"Trouble in paradise, yes?"

"No, well, I don't think so, look, Cathy, when I first started work with Mark and Tony I was given an infinity pool to design."

"What the hell is an infinity pool, Lia?"

"It's a pool without an edge; it's built usually on a slope so the pool looks like it goes on forever; it's clever and relaxing; the water one side tips over and disappears down into a smaller pool below and the water is pumped back so it flows all the time if you're in the pool. And if you're near the sea, if you're clever at designing it, you can make it look like it is part of the sea itself and I did my best, sent the design and this man went with my idea and he had it built on the side of the hill at his villa, and yes, it did look like it was part of the actual ocean."

"So you're telling me that the water continually flows around and around, is that what you're saying, Lia?"

"Sort of, well, I did it and sent the designs to Mr Russo Valentino; we talked a lot during the construction and he asked me to come for a visit, I promised, but I never did. I was too busy and have been ever since. He died three months ago and the solicitors that turned up yesterday said I'm in his will."

"So what did he leave you, Lia?"

"I never got that far, I was in tears and feel so guilty, Cathy."

"Look, how many jobs have you done for Mark and Tony, Lia?"

"Lots in the almost six years I have worked for them."

"So if you visited every client you have worked for, Lia, you would not have enough time to actually work, right?"

"I suppose you're right, but it makes me so sad, Cathy." She came back with a jam doughnut, put it in front of her with another tea.

"There, comfort food, eat and work that's the best remedy for sadness and regret." Cathy was right and Lia got on with the work in hand. She went to inspect the penthouse. Alan took her up where the veranda was in; the ornate railings were going in and the floor-to-ceiling glass doors were about to be fitted; Lia had them made so they folded back and were on sliders to bring the outside in. The staircase to the upper floor was in place; it was made of reinforced glass and the steps were in and covered with plastic to protect the glass from being damaged.

"The kitchen is there, but they are coming tomorrow to fit it. Lia, can you check if it's where you want the cabinets to be?" She went in and checked, the layout was perfect. Alan took her back down the stairs; he was the site manager staying on while Lia completed the apartments, and part of the penthouse. The rest of the penthouse was not in her contract.

Her phone rang and she stopped.

"I need to take this, Alan, see you in the office."

"Mr Simons, what can I do for you?"

"I'm sorry I was not in the office when you called, Miss Westlake, can we schedule a meeting please?"

"I do apologise for yesterday, Mr Simons, it was quite a shock that I have been included in Mr Valentino's will. I heard that much, so tell me why have I not had confirmation until now? Three months is an awful long time."

"Look, I know you're are at work, could I come around and explain it to you? I can be there in twenty minutes."

"Yes, but at the moment, it's still a building site. I will meet you at the gate." Twenty minutes later, the eldest solicitor John turned up and Alan gave him a hard hat and escorted him up to Lia's office. Alan opened the door and he walked in. John looked around and he was impressed. He was given a chair, and Cathy came over with a coffee after asking him what drink he wanted.

"I will leave you to talk, Lia, ring me when you have finished."

"Thank you, Cathy, we won't be long." Cathy shut the door quietly.

"So, Mr Simons, tell me please this is not straight forward, is it?"

"I'm afraid not, the head of the Valentino family requests you go to Milan to receive the bequest Mr Russo Valentino left you; the will is being read next week and the whole family will be there."

"Really, well, you have to inform whoever this person is that as you can see I have my hands full here and there is no way I can stop to go to Milan, it's impossible. Besides, I'm not family, I have never been to the residence, I'm afraid, too much work on.

"Is there no way you could delegate for a few days, Miss Westlake, surely you have an assistant? This is very important."

"No, Mr Simons, no assistant, just Cathy, this is my project and mine alone, it's the way I work, and the crucial part of this project is about to start, dressing the six apartments and of course the penthouse that I have just finished altering for my bosses." John was looking at the designs on her desk.

As young as she was, this was a huge project to take on and he realised that there was no way he was getting her to Italy.

"Did you design all the property on this site?"

"No, Mr Simons, a consortium built the block, I just design the inside, and I get to suggest certain design alterations, which if approved, they go ahead."

"Expensive, Miss Westlake."

"Very, Mr Simons, that's why I have no time for Italy, do apologise for me, but I cannot possibly go." John left and went back to his office; he could see Italy was out but would his client see it the way he does? He phones Italy and asks to speak to Senior Dominic Delgado whose mother was Russo Valentino's sister and who inherited the estate. The phone is picked up after a short pause.

"Mr Simons, I assume the young lady is coming to Italy for the will reading?"

"I'm so sorry, Senior Delgado, but the young lady in question is at the moment very busy, and I'm afraid, Italy is out. Miss Westlake is in the middle of designing the complete inside of a building which I was privileged to see for myself; she, I must admit, is very clever. I do apologise that I could not adhere to your instructions."

"Thank you, Mr Simons, for trying. I will have to make other arrangements." The phone went down, and now, Dominic is very angry and he is finding out as much as he can about Miss Lia Westlake. He is straight on the phone to his security in London, he wants a report as soon as possible.

Lia arrives home and Nancy makes her a drink.

"Busy day, Lia?"

"Not really, the solicitor turned up, the older one; he was trying to persuade me to go to Italy." The door opened and her mum walked in.

"Who wants you to go to Italy?"

"Mr Simons came to see me after I tried to see him this morning; he was allowed up to my office where I explained that I could not in any shape or form get to Italy for the will reading; apparently, the whole family would be in attendance."

"So, Lia, did you find out who it is that wants you to attend this will reading?"

"No, Mum, I left it to John Simons to give my apologies, let's hope that's the end of it." Lia went up to change. Donna and Nancy sat drinking tea.

"Do you not think it's strange, Nancy, that the solicitors have been engaged to get Lia out to Italy for this will reading?"

"Actually, I do, it's a client she was engaged to design an infinity pool for, a strange request but she did it."

"Yes, she did, Nancy, and she kept in touch with the client by Skyping and they talked a lot; the pool was built by a company in Italy and he was very pleased with it and Lia's design. I remember he invited her out for a short holiday, but she never made it, too busy, now I think she is sad she never actually met him, but if he left her something in his will, why do they want her to go to Italy for the will reading, surely it concerns the family not a stranger like Lia."

"Maybe she should find out who is insisting she go out to Italy, Donna." The door opened and Lia came in.

"Look, I'm letting sleeping dogs lie, I'm not going there, you two are just curious to see what I have been left, me, I'm not bothered. I'm sad he died, he would have been ninety I think this year sometime; it was a pleasure designing the pool and I was flattered he used my design, but I don't want anything from his will. I designed the pool for him as a favour." Life went back to normal and Lia forgot about the will; she was too busy. Suddenly, the building contractors left and she was dealing with the contractors she hired to deal with the inside of the building; the walls were being painted and wallpaper put up, then the floors were going in, bathrooms being tiled and quarry tiles on the kitchen floors. The kitchens were being fitted and the bathrooms; all six apartments had different kitchens, the bathrooms were basic but the tiles and flooring different. Twelve bathrooms and bedrooms to dress, a fleet of contractors coming and going.

The penthouse was still to be started. Lia was beginning to stress, but she had help in the form of Keith who was helping with the bathroom co-ordinates and the bed linen. The bedroom furniture was sourced from a manufacturer in York, and to get what she wanted, she had to go see for herself. She drove up; she was staying in the Hilton in York for three nights. Lia got there early driving up early hours of the morning; she was registered and directed to the company she was looking for. It was a huge concern, and as she drove up, you could smell the wood. Mr Jameson was waiting for her and Lia had a tour of the factory. The furniture was beautiful and she sat in his office drinking tea, and Mr Jameson came in with his manager; he shook hands with Lia.

"So what are you exactly after?"

"It's a set of luxury apartments, six in total, two bedrooms in each apartment." And she showed them her designs. Mr Jameson could accommodate her, but it would take six weeks and the bedrooms would arrive all at once in three container lorries, also she wanted six dining tables with extensions each one different to match the decor and eight chairs for each apartment, two carvers and six dining chairs, the order came to 2.2 million. She went back to the hotel up to the suite and showered, and room service came with a tray on it, ham sandwiches with a side salad and a pot of tea. Lia had a lay on the bed; she put her phone alarm on. The leather factory would have to wait till tomorrow, she was worn out from driving and touring the factory. Her alarm went off, she got up and phoned her mum.

"How you doing, Lia?"

"Fine, Mum, I have ordered the bedrooms and the dining tables and chairs; the furniture here is beautiful and they are going with my designs. Tomorrow, the leather factory, and I hope what I need."

"What about the penthouse, are you ordering furniture from the factories up there?"

"No, Mum, Tony and Mark are dressing the penthouse so I was told yesterday I'm having nothing to do with it; it is not part of my contract. I have enough to do, I just designed the veranda and the ornate railings, the doors and the windows. I'm going down to dinner another day tomorrow." Lia came out of the lift and she went to the restaurant, the waiter took her over to the window and sat her at a single table. There was another one just along the way. The waiter came up with a bottle of wine Lia approved and he poured her a glass. Suddenly, a man was shown to the single table. Lia was looking at the menu, she never looked up. The waiter came back, she ordered a salmon soufflé, a fish pie with small

Jersey potatoes and peas. The waiter left and she looked up. The man was staring at her and he was good-looking.

"Good evening." He smiled. She smiled back.

"Good evening." The waiter came up with her starter.

"You obviously like fish. I could not help hearing what you ordered."

"You're right, I love fish, but the pie will surface. I had a few sandwiches this afternoon and I needed something not too heavy. I don't care much for meat unless it's well done." He smiled.

"So no steak for you then?" Lia was enjoying the soufflé.

"Seeing as we both seem to be without partners would you care to join me?"

"No, I'm fine where I am, thanks for the offer." The waiter came up with his soup and he proceeded to eat. Lia's main came up and it was delicious, the pastry on the pie was very light and she enjoyed it; she sat back and had another glass of wine. His main came up, steak and all the trimmings. She sat trying to look out the window, but he spoke making her look at him.

"I assume you are not from around here."

"No, I'm from London."

"So you're on holiday, yes?"

"No, a shopping spree. I like York, there are some lovely things to be had here and a lot cheaper than London." She noticed he had finished his steak; she also noticed he was wearing a gold Rolex watch; he obviously had money.

"If you don't think I'm being nosy, where about in London do you come from?"

"Around the Battersea Park area." He looked puzzled.

"I don't think I know that area."

"Really, it's very vibrant, coffee bars and lots to do entertainment wise."

She was getting up when he put his napkin down.

"Please you're not going, it's very early."

"I'm afraid so, I have an early start again in the morning."

"More retail therapy?"

"I'm afraid so, I'm on a tight schedule, a lot to do. I'm here for three nights and then back to London to work. If you'll excuse me; it was nice talking to you." Lia goes up in the lift, she can feel his eyes boring into her back. She makes herself some tea from the hospitality bar, gets in bed and puts her music on. He was very good looking and not English although his accent would make you think he was. Italian came to mind.

The next morning at 7.30, Lia was in the restaurant having breakfast. The waiter came up to her, she ordered cornflakes with peaches and cream, two pieces of toast and a pot of tea.

Suddenly, the man came in the restaurant and a waiter came up to him.

"Senior Delgado, your table is ready if you'll follow me." Lia saw him escorted to a table where a beautiful woman was sitting; he bent and kissed her on the cheek. Definitely foreign, Italian, no doubt. Lia finished and she left the table without him seeing her.

"Waiter, you served a young woman as well as me last night, do you know her name?"

"Sir, she is sitting having breakfast this very minute." But as the waiter pointed, the table was empty.

"Sir, Miss Westlake was, I do believe, going shopping." He tipped the waiter and proceeded to eat his breakfast.

"So, Dominic, apart from sorting the locals out, did the business you come here to investigate work out?"

"As usual, Leonora, no, I will stick with London, but York is a beautiful city."

"Then I will see you at home. I prefer Milan and the villa." He smiled.

"You got the dresses you needed, did you not?"

"Yes, after you persuaded me to come here, I was actually surprised."

"The jet is on standby, when you require it just say and I will see you safely to the airport."

"This afternoon, I will go back to Italy with your permission. I'm not looking forward to the will reading next week; it is so sad, Dominic, but Russo Valentina had a good life, but I will miss him."

"Such is life, Leonora, but remember, Russo Valentino loved the chateau."

"I know and the infinity pool was his favourite past time. I do believe his life was much longer because he liked to swim in the pool. Whatever Russo left the young English girl, she deserves every penny, that pool made him so happy I can't wait to meet her."

Dominic now knew it was not going to happen, but he would meet her, and when he does, she would get her just desserts.

Dominic Delgado had investigated this woman that designed the infinity pool and he had found she was working in London on a building project, he had also made enquiries in York but had investigated a business venture recommended by his best friend Marco but he preferred London to York, but now by sheer coincidence, he had thought he met the woman who made Russo Valentino sad at an incident in his life. Lia arrived at the leather factory and was shown to the manager's office. She had the samples they sent her and the colours she wanted and the leather couches she required, beige, grey, navy blue, black, raspberry and dark green, two of each set slightly different. But she wanted six leather oblong stools in the same colours. The bill came to 750,000 pounds to be delivered in six weeks dead on time.

She decided to go look at the glass factory, she wanted vases, not your usual vases, long thin stem vases as well as big round ones. She walked through marking down what she needed; there was one a big bowl shape, but it had been blown with a pattern of squares. She called a worker over.

"Yes, ma'am, can I help you?" Lia pointed to the big bowl.

"Is it possible to get more of that pattern? I could do with six if it's possible." The guy looked at her.

"Maybe I need to get the foreman." He used his phone and soon two men were walking down the aisle.

"Jack, the lady wants to know if we can get her six of the blocked bowl."

"Of course, ma'am, these are made to order, they are fifteen hundred pounds each."

"In that case, I need to see the rest." He showed her more and Lia ordered over ten thousand pounds worth of glass vases. She also ordered six sets of crystal glasses, all sizes, another four thousand pounds; they would be delivered in seven weeks, perfect. She got back late and had her laptop case as well as a briefcase; she went to reception for her key.

Lia walked to the lift, and as she got in, Dominic got out and stopped the lift door.

"Busy day?"

"Yes. It was fruitful. I got most of what I needed." She smiled and stepped in, he let the door go and she was going up. In the room, she poured herself a glass of wine, she needed it, tomorrow she would be going home a day early done and dusted. She smiled, everything was coming together. She sat and updated the list, the coordinating things like kitchen equipment would be bulk bought. She showered and ordered dinner in her room then went to bed early. The next morning, she sat and updated her laptop so Mark and Tony could see that she had started to buy the furniture for the six apartments and the prices she paid. Tony came in the office; Mark was already in. Janice brought him in a coffee; he booted up his computer and there was the email from Lia with the lists and prices of the things she had bought and when they would be delivered.

"Tony, the email came in from Lia, she has spent a lot of money, the apartments are coming together, we need to get our fingers out, the penthouse needs designing." Tony walked over to Mark's computer and looked.

"Well, there we have a problem the penthouse I have had an offer unseen 12 million, but if we go with the offer, it must be ultra-modern as in decor." Mark looked at Tony.

"So, you're telling me we need Lia to design the inside?" said Mark.

"Yes, that's what I'm saying and the owner if we go for it knows what he want."

"Like what, Tony?"

"He is waiting to see if we go for the price, then he will submit the design he wants." Mark is not so sure this is a good idea.

"Lia will not go for it, she agreed to add the veranda and the ornate railings and the doors and windows but that was structural and the builders agreed. Lia is up to her armpits in the apartments. Tony, we agreed to design and decorate the penthouse."

"Look, Mark, we got the building cheap when the original owner got in debt, the building when finished is going to give us a profit however much Lia spends and she is not extravagant, she is a very cute shopper that's why she went to York. Look, please ask her to do the penthouse for us."

"So what if she says no, what then, Tony?"

"You have to change the way you design, Mark."

"And you too, Tony, this is going to be a disaster."

Lia got back from York, she parked up and Nancy opened the front door.

"You're early, you were not due back till tomorrow; did you get everything?" She came in the kitchen and sat down.

"Everything, Nancy, and more. I spent over three million pounds in two days, but I got bargains. I need a shower, see you later." As she left the kitchen, she got an email. Today sent from Mark and Tony. Subject: Penthouse. To: Lia Westlake.

"Lia, we have a buyer for the penthouse but he wants ultra-modern, we were hoping you would oblige and design it for us." She immediately phoned Mark and he answered.

"Look, before you shout, it was Tony who got the offer, not me and it's an opportunity not to miss. He is offering 12 million unseen, Lia, but he wants as we said ultra-modern, part of the deal Tony agreed."

"Tell Tony to go to the library and borrow a book on ultra-modern designs, the book will give him ideas. I'm too busy, sorry, no." She put the phone down.

"What did she say, Mark?"

"She suggested you go get a book on ultra-modern designs from the library and study, she said no." The next morning in her makeshift office on site, the boys turned up, she knew they would come, she was waiting for them. Cathy made them coffee and left Lia to it.

"So, tell me do you two ever do any work now or is it just me?"

"Lia, please, you know we employed you because you brought the company up into the 21st century, our designs are not what the client wants."

"So, you sit back and let me do all the work because everyone wants ultra-modern, no, it's your contract your responsibility, I'm finishing the apartments so get your fingers out and start designing."

"Look, he wants you that's his preference, sorry, Lia."

"So, who is he, Tony, you're dealing with?"

"Some rich billionaire who wants a pad in London."

"So, he is staying a mystery." Tony came over to her laptop and punched a file in and opened it. She looked and the designs he wanted was out of this world. The veranda itself was to be sheltered with white sails in resin and a jacuzzi and sun beds and flower boxes. The lounge open plan with huge white couches, coffee tables and the floor shimmering with dark brown tiles. Lia thinks he has visited the penthouse because he agrees with the kitchen being stainless steel, but

23

he wants a breakfast bar in the kitchen and four tall stools. The dining room the table has to be glass edged with mahogany and ten chairs again in colour to match the table, the walls very light, the sideboard that will run down one wall also mahogany but glass fronts to display the crockery and other things. The lighting to be discreet and shaded in the room. One of the other rooms to be decked out as a cinema and games room; he wants music throughout the penthouse installed all around sound. The bedrooms two for guests on the upper floor, the designer can choose the decor, master bedroom a five foot bed is needed, a walk-in wardrobe and in the bathroom a his and hers identical basins, a sunken bath, bidet, and the shower must be big and the decor black and white tiles with a granite unit in black and white to house the hand bowls. Water full taps and a white cupboard to house towels and toiletries. He insists on a full-length mirror in the wardrobe and the mirrors in the bathroom edged with black and white to match. Lia looks the shower alone will set them back ten thousand pounds. The person insists the master bedroom has Egyptian silk sheets in two colours, black and green, the floor mahogany and the drapes at the window slide shut, no nets of any kind in the penthouse. Downstairs, the smallest room is to be carpeted and painted with pale green walls and left. The entrance to the penthouse is a square hall entered via the lift, a table will be delivered, it's to be treated very carefully, it's a 17th century antique. Lia looks away, she is shocked.

"So, how long have we got, Tony, to do all this?"

"You have eight weeks, but we will help, promise."

"Not long enough, I need ten weeks, some of the things I bought will take seven weeks to get here, I'm not a machine."

"Okay, I will get him to agree to ten weeks."

"Tony, you tell him ten weeks or he goes elsewhere." They decide to send Terry and Naomi to help plus the electrics are being sourced out to an expert company employed by Mr Delgado. Tony and Mark agreed to get the kitchen equipment from the retailers Lia recommended, for all the property. The cushions for the apartments have been commissioned from the company Lia's best friend July runs; she need to see her for the penthouse. She reluctantly agrees to take command, but they owe her big time. Her phone goes and Lia looks, it's the solicitors.

"Miss Westlake, we heard from Italy and there is a sum of one million pounds left to you and you will be receiving it in due course. Mr Alfonso's nephew regrets you could not attend but understands."

"Mr Simons, I can't possibly accept such a sum of money."

"I'm afraid, you have no choice, but it will be sometime before you receive the money. I suggest you then discuss it with the representative." Lia puts the phone down, she decides to discuss it with no one, not even her mum until she knows more. With the painting, wallpapering and the floors laid, the first apartment has the kitchen installed and the bathroom. Lia goes up to the penthouse, the place has been cleaned and the sails are going up, a team were at work putting the electrics in and Tony is overseeing it, at least he is doing something to help. Then Lia realises that the company fitting the electrics are not your usual electricians, this company Lia knew what they did. The company dealt with security on a grand scale, not the usual kind houses had installed. Suddenly, there is a man by her side.

"Ma'am, we are installing the security systems, there will be a panel by the door to the penthouse, when it's up, I will show you."

"So, are these men putting the sound system in as well?"

"Yes, ma'am, it will run off a computer set in the office."

"What office?" He took Lia along to the small room past the games room, it was knitted out as an office desk chair, cabinets and all the electronic gadgets a modern office would have. She was convinced the person who had bought the penthouse was around somewhere. At least one room she would not have to worry about. Gradually over two weeks with twelve men working on the decorating, it was almost finished, the floor layers were in, the tiling in the first two apartments complete and the bathrooms going in the showers were up, just the electrics and the down lighters to be completed. Lia decided to take the next day off to shop her favourite part of the job; she took her laptop and went to see Judy, her friend who ran her own company designing soft furnishings, who she had an order with when she needs her help. Lia walks in the factory and suddenly Judy is hugging her.

"So you decided to visit instead of doing business over the phone?"

"Sorry, Judy, it's easier that way, besides you know exactly what I need, but I'm in trouble and needed to see you face to face." The door opens and a girl comes in with tea and she leaves. Lia gets her laptop out, turns it on and puts it on Judy's desk and brings up the pictures up. She looks.

"Wow, what's that, not one of your projects?"

"Afraid so, Tony and Mark lumbered me with the penthouse."

"I thought you had the six apartments and them the penthouse?"

"Apparently, the owner wants 21st century modern, not old-fashioned Victorian splendour."

"I see and Tony and Mark are out of their comfort zone, right?"

"Not only am I lumbered but I have sourced all the furniture and the glass I need in York the other week, now I have to start again, what the hell do I do!" Lia takes her through the actual penthouse showing her the type of theme the owner wants.

"Look, let's go see Ben, he has his own furniture-making company, he fits bespoke bedrooms, he can help. The couches can be found in the exotic leather company. Ben can get hold of antique coffee tables and I will sort out the soft furnishings for the bedrooms and lounge."

"Let's go see Ben." Ben is a forty-year-old married man with three children and an expert in building furniture who at the moment was not that busy and could do with the work. So, Lia takes Judy and Ben to the apartments and they go up in the lift to the penthouse. The team are still there fitting the electrics and suddenly Tony comes out the office, he is talking to someone, he turns and sees Lia.

"I thought you were out for the day, what are you doing up here?"

"What do you think, since when do I have to ask permission to walk on to my own job?" Suddenly, the office door opens and Lia recognises the man from the hotel in York.

"Small world, now everything makes sense, if you'll excuse me." She walks up the stairs with Ben and Judy and Tony is just standing there. They go into the first bedroom.

"A guest room and the next." Ben measures up and Judy and Lia sit in the bathroom.

"What's with the guy in the room, Lia, are you okay, you looked like you have seen a ghost."

"Not a ghost but things have been happening that I can't work out, Judy, and it's beginning to make me uneasy. Look, I saw him in York, he was in the same hotel as me then I saw him the day I was coming home having breakfast with someone."

"Male or female?"

"Female, she was already at the table, he joined her." Suddenly, he walked in the bedroom and Ben called her, she walked out.

"I was wondering if before you leave I could have a word with you, please, Miss Westlake."

She went to refuse when Judy piped up,

"Don't worry about us, Tony will give us a lift, right, Tony?" Tony had just walked in the bedroom.

"Sure, when you're ready, give me a shout." The man and Tony walked out together.

"He fancies you, Lia, and he has beautiful green eyes, what's his name?"

"That's it, I have no idea, we have spoken he has never told me his name."

"Yet he knows who you are, strange, don't you think, Ben?" They were in the master bedroom and Ben looked at the drawings.

"Dark rosewood, Lia, then you can co-ordinate the other furniture, make it slightly lighter, what do you think?"

"That would be perfect, Ben, and the walk-in wardrobe the colour inside I was thinking beige, you're going to need it light." Suddenly, she realised he was at the door with Tony.

"Mr Johnson, perfect, I will leave it up to you." Lia just stood there, she was having a word with Tony. They walked down the stairs.

"Why glass, Lia, I must say they are beautiful," said Ben.

"I want them to stay that way so you look through them, Ben, can you make slip-proof inserts so no one falls down them?"

"Yes, no problem, I need to get to the tread to measure."

Tony came up to Lia. "Mr Delgado is waiting for you, I will take Judy and Ben back, you need to…"

"Really and why, Tony, why is he here, and why was he in the same hotel as me in York?"

"Look, we are going to go see him, please, a lot is riding on you getting on with him." She knocked on the door, suddenly he opened the door.

"Miss Westlake, at last we need to talk." She walked in and sat on a chair; he walked around and sat at the desk.

"So, tell me in the scheme of things, Miss Westlake, where do you come in this project?" Lia thought this was a question that seemed to have challenging answers.

"Me? I'm the designer and therefore responsible for the way the project goes."

"Well, I'm representing the family investing in this penthouse. I too have a lot of responsibility. I recommended the penthouse to the family."

"So why twelve million, you could have got it for less, if you waited for it to be finished."

"The family decided an abode in London was essential and as I have business here I volunteered to oversee the project as you call it, trust me they can afford it, and they know what they want and the security was essential." She stood up, she was going; he wanted her to stay; she put her hand out.

"Thank you for explaining, now I really have to go. I assume you will be here keeping your eye on the project." He smiled.

"Please have dinner with me, we almost did at the hotel in York."

"Separate tables as I remember, sorry, I have still got work to complete at the office. I will see you around, and just so you know, I do not mix work with pleasure and you and the penthouse is work so if you'll excuse me." She left down in the lift and was driving away. Judy was right, he had beautiful grey-green eyes for a man, but she did not trust him, and whatever this was all about, it was for her a job that she needed to complete.

When Lia got back, Cathy had gone. Lia set about putting the furniture into the laptop images she looked she had a penthouse resembling a luxury apartment. She took her laptop and left for home.

Donna was in the kitchen with Nancy when she got in; she went in the kitchen.

"Darling, you look tired, you're working too hard, you need a break. Thank God, the project is nearly over."

"Mum, it's not. I now have the penthouse to furnish and it's being made a lot more difficult because the family that bought it have a representative overseeing the job."

"So, where is Tony and Mark? I thought it was their baby."

"It was, but the family want ultra-modern not Victorian splendour so it falls to me to furnish the penthouse."

"You know, Lia, if you were younger, I would give them what, for they are taking the Mickey, you have six two-bedroom luxury apartments to design, all they had was the penthouse."

"And that's not all, Mum, what makes me so angry, Mum, is that they sold the penthouse for 12 million and it includes this makeover and the man has installed an office in the small lounge and there is security on a large scale, you would think they were housing the Crown Jewels in the penthouse, then there is around sound going in and God knows what else, and what is strange is that when I was in York staying at the hotel the same man was having dinner at the table next to me and then there is the will. I'm beginning to think there is a conspiracy going on and it's making me feel uncomfortable."

"So, how long will it take to complete, Lia?"

"Ten weeks. I have got Judy on board, she introduced me to Ben, he makes bespoke furniture and he is doing the bedrooms and the master bedroom, but I have a feeling there is a lot more to this job that I have no idea about, and it has me looking over my shoulder and I have no idea why."

"Lia, just finish the six apartments and leave the rest to Tony and Mark. You're not a machine, Lia, they are not playing fair with you."

"Tomorrow, I'll go to the Exotic Leather Company for the couches for the main lounge." Nancy put a lasagne in front of her with a salad and she dug in, she was hungry as she had missed lunch. The next day, Judy met her at the leather warehouse and it was huge; the furniture was more expensive than York, but she needed six couches but went with four after advice from the director and four armchairs, the couches in white as requested and the chairs in dark brown. Sitting them in the lounge on her laptop, they looked spectacular.

For the next week, Lia was in the penthouse, but Mr Delgado was nowhere to be seen and Lia felt better and got on with the job in hand; the painters were in and the kitchen was installed, the bathroom was being tiled in black and white in the master bedroom, lemon and white in one guest bathroom, a sea green and white in the other guest bathroom. On Friday, Tony and Mark showed up, with Mr Delgado and they were showing him what had been achieved and he was thanking them. Lia was in the master bedroom overseeing the painters when they walked in; they had no idea she was in the penthouse; they both looked guilty.

"We recommended this colour, a hint of red to lighten the room up, a good colour to go with the mahogany furniture, Mr Delgado, don't you think?" He looked at Lia and smiled. Lia turned.

"Yes, I totally agree, definitely what I would have chosen, don't you agree, Miss Westlake?"

"Can I have a word please, Mark, now?" Lia walked out the bedroom and Tony stayed with Mr Delgado.

"So, what's going on? All week you were nowhere to be seen and suddenly you're making out as if it's all your work, why?" Mark looks guilty.

"So, I do all the donkey work and you take the praise, right?" She knows by his face something is not right. She goes back in the bedroom and talks to the painters, then she immediately packs up her things. She takes her laptop and begins to walk out the bedroom; the painters are finishing the wall and are finishing up for the day. Tony follows her out the bedroom.

"What going on, Lia?"

"All yours, Tony, I quit. I should have never agreed to take the penthouse on. I'm going to the office, collect my things and I'm leaving your baby, you finish it." She walks out down in the lift and gets in the car. She finally drives off when she has her anger under control, she does not want an accident. She walks up the steps. July is typing up the lists of furniture she has commissioned for the penthouse; she gets her to print off the pictures; she will give them at least the designs.

"Lia, are you okay?" July can see tears; she comes over to her.

"No, I'm leaving, sorry, July, I won't be back. They made a fool of me in front of Mr Delgado. I have no idea what's going on and now I don't care, nobody does that and gets away with it, sorry." She walks down the stairs and drives away. Twenty minutes later and July has finished typing up the bills and the door opens and Tony walks in.

"Lia been back, July?" She can see he is stressing.

"You know she has been here." July give Tony the printed version of her designs where everything in the penthouse will go; she can see by his face he is shocked.

"What the hell happened?"

"She came in here; she was so angry she said you made a fool out of her and nobody does that and gets away with it. That girl was actually crying. I personally think you have lost her, Tony. Here is the list of furniture she has commissioned and the leather couches and armchairs bought. You now have six apartments and a penthouse to dress, good luck."

"You walking out too, July?"

"I don't actually work for you. I'm helping or was helping Lia so I guess the answer's yes."

"Please stay, we need to apologise to Lia, God, this is a mess."

"Okay, I will be here in the morning as usual. I hope you find someone for me to work with." She stood waiting.

"I need to lock up, Tony, take what you need or I'm on overtime." He went down got in the car, his phone rang.

"Did you get her, Tony?"

"No, she has gone but left us the designs. See you at the office, we need a plan B and urgently." Lia got home; she parked up, tears were falling down her face. She sat there until she got herself under control. Her phone rings, a number she does not recognise.

"Look, if you're selling anything, I'm not interested, sorry."

"Delgado here, Miss Westlake, what's going on, you walked out on the job.

"I want to know why."

"Talk to Tony and Mark Grossman and Partner. I no longer work for them."

"Miss Westlake, we need to talk. I'm afraid, the contract I signed included you and it's legal I made sure of it."

"I never signed a contract with you, Mr Delgado, sorry not my problem."

"The contract says Grossman and Partner and assistant Miss Lia Westlake, that's you, either you work as the contract states or I will sue Mr Grossman and Partner, your choice."

"As I said, Mr Delgado, not my problem. I never agreed to anything to do with the penthouse."

"But you did the apartments, it was your contract and I have both now. I will pick you up at 7.30, be ready, you and I are now going to dinner. We need to talk, Miss Westlake, and I will not take no as an answer." He discontinued the call. Lia walked indoors and her mum came up to her.

"You were in the car talking for a long time, everything okay, Lia?"

"Fine, Mum, I need to shower I'm going out to dinner at 7.30." She walked upstairs and Nancy could see Lia was upset.

"Out to dinner I wonder who with, Nancy?" At 7.30, Donna got her answer, at the door was a man whose looks would take your breath away.

"Lia's mother, I assume, it's nice to meet you. Mr Delgado at your service."

"Do come in, Mr Delgado, I will tell Lia you're here." Suddenly, she is coming down the stairs and her mother is in shock. Lia has a dress on that is beautiful and her hair is left loose and she held it back with two diamond combs. She puts her jacket on and stands in the hall. Donna can see Mr Delgado is as shocked as her.

"So, are we going to dinner, Mr Delgado, you instigated this, not me." Donna is shocked as he tries to take Lia's arm, but Lia walks to the car and the chauffeur gets out, opens the door and Lia gets in. Delgado gets in through the other side and they drive away.

"A beautifully attired woman and a very angry voice not a good combination, I'm afraid."

"Tuff, you instigated this dinner I'm adhering to your demand that's all, so let's get on with it, shall we?" The chauffeur is enjoying this, his boss is at a loss as what to do. They get to the hotel, he escorts her in and the waiter shows them to a table in the middle of the restaurant. Lia will have to behave, the restaurant is very busy. The waiter takes her jacket and sits her down.

"So, what would you like to drink, Lia?"

"White wine please." The waiter returns with a bottle. Delgado tries it and approves and the waiter pours her a glass; she sips it and it's nice.

"So, shall we order, Lia, talk after, yes?"

"Your date, not mine, fine." Lia orders a salmon soufflé and for main she wants an Italian shrimp and scampi pasta salad. He orders the same.

"So before we eat, I'm sorry, Lia, if I may call you that, I had no idea you never saw the contract but you did sign the contract to design and furnish the apartments, did you not?"

"Yes, I did, but with Tony and Mark, not you. Again, I'm not too happy with the situation, but I will complete the apartments. I was too hasty, but I'm having my lawyers make sure it's legal."

"Well, I will be satisfied with at least one contract being completed, but the penthouse had to be the crowning glory, Lia, and with you, it will be just that so can you not work your magic for me? The penthouse needs you." She smiled; Dominic was looking at a breath-taking woman.

The food arrived and Lia was enjoying the food and her glass seemed to be full all the time.

"What made you go into designing, Lia?" He needed her talking, he needed to see if the harsh way Russo spoke about this woman warranted what he intended doing to her.

"I loved drawing and I loved designing right from middle school. When I went to university, I excelled and passed all the exams and read a lot about different types of furniture through the ages and examples of Victorian art and crafts."

"So, why ultra-modern designs, not that I'm knocking it, I like modern and Victorian, and being Italian, I like the very old-fashioned furniture as well. I know you like perfection. I have been, let me say, checking you out and I'm sure you would hate the penthouse to not come up to your expectation, right?"

"I suppose so, Mr Delgado, so what are you trying to say?"

"Lia, finish the penthouse for me and make Tony and Mark your assistants, that way the project would be perfect. I must say the owner insists on Venetian glass around the penthouse so someone has to go to Venice to purchase the glass needed, do you think Tony or Mark are up to the job?" Lia was on her third glass of wine, she had finished her meal and the waiter was clearing away.

"The dessert trolley, sir, would you like me to bring it up?"

"So, Lia, will you indulge in a dessert?" She smiled, she was beginning to like him. Suddenly, the dessert trolley appeared and the mouth-watering desserts were in front of her. She chose a strawberry tart with cream and Delgado a slice of chocolate gateaux.

"So, you like strawberries, maybe I will order champagne and strawberries, see if you like a combination drink."

37

"Please another time. I have had enough wine, can I have a cup of tea, please?"

"Waiter, tea for the lady and coffee for me. So, you have just stated you will have dinner with me again. I look forward to it." He smiled. They left the table and went in the lounge. He sat her down; the chairs were very comfortable.

"So, you never answered my question about the Venetian glass."

"Tony and Mark would love to go to Venice, but knowing what to buy, you have not a hope in hell. I have worked for them for six years and I always put the finishing touches even to their projects; it makes the project complete."

"So, would you consider me escorting you to Venice to buy the glass pieces on behalf of the family?"

"No, not necessary, there is a thriving business in Venetian glass here in London, very expensive but beautiful. In fact, it's not too far away from here. If you like, I could take you, just say the word." He smiled; he has her.

"Tell me, Mr Delgado, why did you buy the whole building before it's finished, because Tony and Mark still have to finish the project."

"The family decided that as they bought the penthouse it was sensible to also control the rest of the building, so six luxury apartments were deemed not a problem to purchase, and of course, Grossman and Partner were quick to sell but with the whole block completed. The contracts still stand, so we have agreed. I'm sorry you should have been in on the meeting; nothing will change until the project is finished, and the whole block is approved by the family and they take charge of the properties. More tea or do you want to go home?"

Lia needed to go home. He was good, very good; he now has persuaded her to complete the penthouse with Tony and Mark, her assistants, this was going to be difficult. He escorted her to the car and they got in. She sat looking out the window, she could see his reflection. She turned, he was looking at her.

"Tell me, Mr Delgado, who is this family that have paid such a high price for the penthouse and apartments?"

"I'm not at liberty to say, but on the launch night, you will obviously meet them. So, I have your word you will complete the contract and I will be having words with your bosses."

"One word of warning, Mr Delgado, any interference from Tony or Mark and I walk. I want my designs back as well by 4 pm tomorrow." They were at her home; he got her out the car and escorted her up to the door. Suddenly, he bent his head and kissed her. Then he walked away.

"Good night, Lia, thank you for a wonderful evening." He was in the car; she closed the front door and heard the car pull away. When Donna got up, Lia was gone and Nancy was making another pot of tea.

"She had a wonderful time last night and is back working, I assume." July was shocked to see Lia walk in the office; she quickly made her a cup of tea.

"What happened, Lia?"

"I had dinner with Mr Delgado last night, and I'm finishing the apartments."

"And the penthouse, Lia?"

"Yes, that too but with no interference from Tony or Mark though."

"You know, they have not got a clue they were going for plan B, whatever that was." She smiled. July and Lia got to the building and into the first apartment, all decorated and the floors were now being laid, the bathroom was in and the kitchen, both tiled and the floors finished. The last flat was now having the bathroom tiled, the kitchen was still being completed and then tiled. They were on schedule a week and the furniture should be arriving, the bedrooms first, the four-man crew have to assemble twelve beds; the rest of the furniture was assembled. They had to get out the last two apartments lounge, and the hall floor was being laid and it would take two days to dry. As they were walking out to reception, Tony and Mark were walking in. Lia ignored them. Tony looked back. Lia could see he was stressed; she felt guilty.

"Look, Lia, let them sweat, you know and so do I, they were up to their necks and drowning, let Mr Delgado tell them what's happening. Just get on and do what you do best, complete the job your way." Back at the office, Lia got in touch with Judy.

"That company that sold Venetian glass, is it still trading?"

"Yes, want to take a look, just say and I will be there, so you're still working for them, Lia?"

"I'm completing the contract, that's all, Judy."

"I see, well, let me know when the drapes need fitting, I will be there." July made tea and she did some filing. There was nothing to do so they both decided to have an early day; it was 2 pm. July went off and Lia drove home; she got in and her mum was surprised to see her.

"For once, I have nothing to do, so I'm home."

"You okay, darling?"

"Not really, you know, when you're on holiday and the last day arrives and you suddenly want to leave, well, I felt like that when July and I were leaving the apartments this morning. Tony and Mark were walking in and we passed each other like strangers and I suddenly did not want to be there anymore. Six years and it comes to this, why did I work so hard for them to stab me in the back, Mum? I agreed to finish the penthouse but I still think there is something not right and it has me worried."

"Darling, are you sure that's what is happening?"

"Mr Delgado has a contract for the penthouse, Tony and Mark's name Grossman and Partner and assistant Miss Lia Westlake. They signed the contract. The contract for the apartments, Mr Delgado has that as well and I signed that so I'm completing the contract then I'm leaving."

"I'm so sorry, Lia, whatever they are up to why did they let Mr Delgado buy the contract, there must be a good reason. It means the whole building now belongs to Mr Delgado, right?"

"Or the family he is working for. So, he bought the apartments as well as the penthouse. So, that means there will be no launch, they are already sold."

"Looks that way, Lia."

"Mum, this is so confusing and I was feeling sorry for them but not anymore. I suppose I will get paid for all the work I have done." Lia gets her contract out on completion, she will earn two million pounds bonus. She rings July and tells her she has the rest of the week off and that she will see her Monday morning early as the bedrooms will be arriving. Lia takes the day off and goes to see Judy.

"Heard anything, Lia?"

"I saw them yesterday walking in the building as July and I were leaving, you would think we were strangers. For six years, Judy, I worked for them and they do this to me, why?"

"Did what, Lia?"

"Sold the whole building to Mr Delgado or the family he is working for."

"Have you googled Mr Delgado, Lia, he is a billionaire, hard to find but I was curious. Fortune speaks for itself; he comes from Italy, Milan actually, but he has businesses in London and he is here often, Lia, and the building you were contracted to complete he bought outright two months ago."

"So, he has a family, right?"

"No, he is according to the Italian Celebrity Magazine quite a catch, but as of yet, he has not been caught. He's a hit with the ladies and has them lining up, but he is discrete according to the magazine and the women he goes out with are the same; there are no nasty rumours about him."

"So now we have discovered as much as we can about the enemy, what can I do for you, Lia?"

"Can you take me to see the factory? I'm maybe looking for Venetian glass, July, he wanted me to go to Venice with him and that's one thing I'm not doing, it's not in the contract; anything not in the contract, I'm not doing." They arrived at this company, very upmarket, the glass on display was beautiful and very expensive. Venetian glass was also called Murano Glass so Lia would have to discuss the problem with Mr Delgado if and when the penthouse was dressed. She phoned Ben from her car; he was well into the bedrooms; he had taken back a few workers. The treads for the stairs were in hand. She decided to go to the building as she wanted to do a walkthrough with her laptop. She got out the lift into the hall, a man was sitting in a chair reading a newspaper.

"Ma'am, I think you're in the wrong place, this is a private penthouse."

"Yes, I know. I'm Lia Westlake the designer, can you let me in?"

"You need a security pass, I'm afraid, if one has not been issued, then no, sorry, you're not allowed in." Suddenly, the door opened and a woman came out followed by Mr Delgado.

"Johnson, this is Lia Westlake, she will need a security pass; she is furnishing the penthouse." He walked along the hallway towards the lift.

"Dominic darling, is she not too young for such an important job? There is a lot of money involved."

"Elena, I know what I'm doing, trust me." Lia turned as Johnson gave her a security number and he let her in. She decided to do a walkthrough. She went in each room and put the furniture where she wanted it. The kitchen was in and the breakfast bar, the stools were there but not unwrapped, just the basic kitchen; there was a lot to do. She walked up the stairs, next week the treads would be in. The bedrooms were painted, the floors to be laid, the bathrooms in place, but the tiles were still in boxes. In the master bedroom, the walls were painted, one wall was left bare as the wallpaper was not yet chosen. She heard a noise and came down the stairs; she went towards the green room as she called it and went to knock. A phone rang she stopped.

"Mr Simons, what can I do for you? I'm sorry I have been very busy. I should have rung you, I apologise."

"I have it in hand. Miss Westlake will get the inheritance from Senior Russo Valentino in due course, thank you for your help in the matter, but I'm in England and can myself see she gets the money. I will be sending you a cheque for your help and thank you again." Lia walks through into the lounge, she has her laptop on, she was going to delete everything and was about to press delete when he walked in. He stopped Lia.

"Lia, you're still here, can I be of assistance?" She just sat there not wanting to even look at him. He came towards her.

"Lia, are you okay, can I offer you tea?" She looked up at him.

"Sorry, I was far away, no, thank you, I was just doing a walkthrough and I needed to tell you I went to look at the glass you say the family want. I need to know exactly what I need to get; it is very expensive, Mr Delgado."

"Please call me Dominic, you heard Elena call me so when you were getting your security clearance, so can I see what you intend on doing with this place?"

"Not yet, I'm not very happy as the master suite has not got its feature wall up yet. Tony was supposed to organise it."

"Look, come back to the office, Lia, and I will ring him and may be you could do with a drink."

"I'm driving home." She looked at her watch. He picked her laptop up. "Come, I will make you tea or coffee." She followed him into the office. He put the laptop on his desk and came back with tea for her and a coffee.

"That was quick." He just smiled. He got on the phone.

"Mr Grossman, I have Lia here in the penthouse and she tells me the feature wall in the master bedroom has not been completed, can you tell me why?" There is a pause as he listens then he disconnects the call.

"He tells me you had the bedrooms painted so he expected you to see to the feature wall."

"Fine, so I will sort it out. I need to go, I'm glad I did a walkthrough. I now know what I'm up against."

"Look, it's the weekend soon, will you have dinner with me Saturday night, Lia? I know a great place to have dinner and there is dancing, what do you say, you did agree to have dinner with me again, remember? Champagne with strawberries." She smiled, but he was irresistible and he knew it.

"Okay, Saturday night but this is the last time."

"I will pick you up at 7 pm if that's okay." She got up and walked to the door.

"Saturday night, 7 pm, till then, Mr Delgado."

"It's Dominic, Lia. I can't wait." Lia sat in the car trying to get her head around the fact he was related some way to Russo Valentino. She drove home. Nancy was in the kitchen cooking when her mum came in.

"Lia, Tony rang you. I told him you were at work, he seemed surprised and asked me to ask you to ring him." Lia sat, drank a cup of tea, then she walked into the lounge. She rang him.

"Lia, I'm sorry about the feature wall in the master bedroom."

"Don't worry about it, I have it in hand, like everything else you seem to not want to do."

"Look, I'm so sorry, but Mr Delgado made us an offer we could not refuse; he was desperate to get the whole building. Mark and I thought he was crazy to offer us twelve million for the penthouse, but then he offered us five million for each apartment on the understanding we left the whole building for you to furnish. We could not refuse, Lia, but we will be helping you in any way we can."

45

"Look, okay, Tony, maybe I believe you. I have no idea what's going on and it's creepy. The bedroom furniture comes Monday, be there to help please."

"Will do, and Lia, I'm so sorry, but we will see you, right, okay." Lia came back in the kitchen.

"Lia, are you okay?"

"No, Mum, I'm thinking this job is getting uncomfortable."

"Then leave it to Tony and Mark, walk away."

"I can't, I'm locked into a contract that now belongs to the man I had dinner with the other night and I think he has something to do with Russo Valentino."

"The man who left you money in his will?"

"Yes, I overheard a conversation, he was talking to Mr Simons the solicitor; he said as he was now in England he would see I got the money."

"Lia, walk away, darling, the money is not worth it, how dare he interfere in your career, and shame on Tony and Mark surely as a businessmen they must have thought it strange a man would pay twelve million pounds for a penthouse before it has been furnished."

"Mum, he bought the apartments for five million each and so I have to complete the furnishing of the apartments, it's in the contract I signed. I now agreed to dress the penthouse and go to dinner with him Saturday night."

"Who the hell is this man, Lia?"

"Well, he has more money than sense; he is supposed to be a businessman according to Judy; she got some celebrity magazine; it was in Italian. He is single and I think all this stems from Russo Valentino and his will, and I'm scared,

Mum, I'm not in control and my head just keeps going around and around."

"Why does that not surprise me, Lia?"

"Mum, he is a billionaire, lives in Milan, and I now know he has something to do with the late Russo Valentino, and his first name is Dominic."

"I'm not happy with this situation, Lia, you be very careful."

"Mum, I'll be twenty-seven in two months 'time and I have July with me all the time, and I now have Ben, Judy's friend, in the penthouse building the bedrooms, and Judy is doing the soft furnishings and Cathy my security."

"So, they going to dinner with you on Saturday?"

"No, Mum, they were not invited, just me."

"Okay, when I'm out, I will get you a pepper spray to keep in your bag, just to be on the safe side. I thought he was nice now I'm not so sure, Lia, cancel the dinner please." Her mum left the kitchen and Nancy gave her a mug of tea.

"What do you think, Nancy?"

"I'm not sure, Lia, you never had dealings with this man when you designed the infinity pool for Senior Valentino, did you?"

"No, the request came in to Mark and he put it on my desk; he said it was more of a challenge than an actual project, but I went to the library and found a book on unusual swimming pools. Nancy, an infinity pool was very new and very expensive and I messed around with drawings."

"So, how did you get in touch with the man?"

"Mark did, by then I had a design even I surprised myself with. Mark sent it to him and we forgot about it, then one day

I got a call, Senior Russo Valentino introduced himself to me. He told me out of all the designs he received he wanted to use mine. I told him I was flattered; he asked me to go out to Italy to oversee the pool. I told him it was not what I did, I designed the inside of apartments, but I had fun designing the pool. I remember it made him laugh. We communicated for nine months why the pool was being erected, Nancy. Senior Valentino paid twenty thousand pounds for the pool and it was my design that started it all off, and I never went out to see it like he asked me to maybe that has something to do with it. I have no idea."

"Lia, how much did you charge him for the design?"

"Nothing, Nancy, it was fun getting all the information I needed on infinity pools. I gave Senior Russo Valentino the design and asked for nothing in return. I was not expecting him to use my design when he said he was going with it. I was flattered and we had fun talking to each other."

"So, that was when, Lia, almost six years ago?"

"Yes, Nancy, why?"

"Nothing, Lia, fancy another cup of tea?" The conversation ended, but Nancy was uneasy and she had no idea why. Lia got a call from Judy and she met her at the apartments; there was a van and Judy was there with Jamie; they got the curtains up in three of the apartments and it was getting late when they finished.

"There're a tiny bit creased, Lia, if it doesn't fall out, I will steam them. Let's hang the next two tomorrow, the last apartment has the floor to set before we can get in." The next day, Lia drove there. Judy arrived and Jamie was up the ladder; it was very tall, the drapes were hung; it was coming together.

"What you wearing for your dinner date tomorrow night, Lia?"

"A sack cloth." Judy laughed.

"Really and you'll look like a dream, I wish I had your figure, Lia."

"Really, Judy, you need to look in the mirror, you have a perfect figure and you know it." Judy hugged her and got in the van with Jamie.

"Let me know what colour sack you're wearing, Lia, I might borrow it." Lia waved as they drove off; she looked up at the penthouse wondering if he was there. She got in her car and drove away.

Saturday morning, she went to the office and phoned the furniture shop in York, the assignment of bedroom suites were on track to leave at 4 am; they were expected in London before 9 am at their destination. Lia thanked them for the information and locked up and went home. Monday was going to be the start of the hard work. She got home after she went to the nail bar, and she walked in. She could hear voices and walked in to the front room. Her mum got up; she recognised the woman sitting there, she had last seen her with Mr Delgado walking out the penthouse.

"Lia, Miss Valentino wanted a word with you, so I will leave you. I will be in the kitchen." Lia took her coat off and sat down. Suddenly, Lia realised this woman was something to do with Russo Valentino.

"So, how did you find out where I lived, Miss Valentino?"

"That was easy, Dominic has a whole security folder on you. In fact, he has your whole life history, Miss Westlake, frightening, isn't it?"

"Why do you say frightening, Miss Valentino, I'm a designer that just happens to be designing a set of apartments Dominic, as you called him now, owns."

"You have no idea, do you, Miss Westlake, do you still intend going to dinner with him tonight and do you still intend finishing the apartments?"

"What the hell has it got to do with you, may I ask?"

"You have no idea, do you? Dominic is a man who does not suffer fools easy and you are, I'm afraid, a fool. If you have any sense, you will get out while you can. I will give you three million dollars to walk away from this project and not look back."

"Do you think I'm a threat to you, Miss Valentino, well, I'm not interested in Dominic Delgado, never was. I'm finishing the job whether you like it or not so I suggest you leave this house and I also suggest you never come back." The woman got up, she walked out the house and got in a car and then drove away. Lia went in the kitchen.

"You okay, Lia, do you want a drink?"

"Please, Nancy, tea." The door opened and her mum walked in.

"So, what was that all about? That woman has been here an hour waiting for you; we gave her coffee and she just made small talk, she said she needed to talk to you; she had something to give you."

"Yes, she offered me three million pounds to walk away from the project, Mum, she is something to do with Russo Valentino, why, I have no idea."

"Why, Lia, you know may be you should work out exactly what is this job when completed worth because it's you doing all the work, not Mark and Tony, maybe you need to step aside, just leave. This man Dominic Delgado I think is whatever is going on is to blame, darling, I'm beginning to think this job is not worth the stress it's putting on you."

"You're not going to believe this, but Dominic Delgado paid forty million for six apartments and a penthouse."

"Okay, so, Lia, what is the overall cost of designing and furnishing the whole block, the penthouse will cost five million to furnish the apartments about two and a half million each. So, that's twenty million. So, say the block cost three million to build, that's twenty-three million Tony and Mark are making, seventeen million mostly on you, Lia."

"Mum, they have to pay me two million, it's in my contract, so that knocks them down to fifteen million then they have the staff wages to pay. It works out right, this was a big money spinning job from the start, the only difference being they were seeing to the penthouse but now it's my baby. I need to get ready for this damn dinner date."

When Lia came down, she looked exquisite, the dress fitted her to perfection. It was completely plain, a pale green silk dress; it hugged her figure and came just below her knees, tiny diamond straps held it up, a pale green belt with a diamond pattern went around her waist changing the dress into a classic fitted dress; she had a jacket, pale green sandals and a bag to match; she clipped her hair up with two huge slides and she was ready. Dead on 7 pm, there was a knock on the door and Nancy opened the door, there stood Mr Delgado; he walked in and Donna came out the lounge.

"Good evening, Mrs Westlake, such a nice evening, don't you think."

"Mr Delgado, I expect my daughter back at a reasonable hour, and as you are taking her to dinner, I'm making you responsible for her; this project Lia has undertaken is getting beyond a joke on one girl, and I don't care how good she is, and my daughter is very good at what she does; she deserves more support than you or Mr Grossman and Partner are giving her as you're in charge now I suggest you do something about it." Lia came out the kitchen.

"You have to excuse my mother, she is annoyed at the visitor we had today, that's all." She walked to the door.

"Mum, I'm able to look after myself and I will see you later." She walked out with Dominic to the car. Jim opened the door; they got in. Lia slipped the seatbelt around herself. They drove off, but Lia looked out the window and not at him, and he was annoyed.

"So, Miss Westlake, what was that all about?"

"Nothing that concerns you, my mother was just being protective, that's all." Lia sat looking out the window again, total silence in the car and Jim was wondering how this evening was going to end. They arrived at the hotel and Jim opened the door. Lia got out and Dominic came around and took her arm and escorted her in; the atmosphere was frosty. They walked in the lounge. Dominic sat her down and a waiter came up.

"What would you like to drink, Lia?"

"A glass of white wine, please." He rattled a name off and the waiter left. The waiter uncorked the bottle and Dominic tasted it, nodded and the waiter poured her a glass, and Dominic then left the bottle in the wine cooler.

"From the conversation your mother was having with me, she thinks you are working too hard, do you always discuss your work with your mother?" She looked up at him and sipped her wine tentatively. He watched her. Lia decided not to answer the question.

"This is a beautiful hotel, very overrated in my opinion, a place where people who need to be seen are seen." She looked at him.

"So, you design beautiful apartments, Lia, but you do not appreciate beautiful surrounding when it comes to yourself, strange, I would have thought a hotel like this would be to your liking."

"For dinner, maybe once in a while, but this type of hotel does not impress me."

"Just as well, we are only having dinner, shall we go? I have booked a private room so we can eat and talk. I think you and I have a lot to talk about after your mother's outburst." Lia is escorted through the lounge and into a room with a table beautifully laid.

"Sir, when shall we serve dinner?"

"Say thirty minutes, can we have another bottle of the same wine, please?"

The waiter left. He was back with the second bottle of wine.

"So, if you have issues, Lia, I need to know. I thought you were happy with the apartments and the penthouse."

"Tell me if you're such a brilliant businessman and we all know you're successful, why did you pay over the odds for the block of apartments and the penthouse?"

"Who says I paid over the odds?"

"I do remember I did the sums, the building, the alterations, the furnishing of the apartments and now the penthouse, you will be out of pocket, especially with the penthouse."

"We will see. I think you will be surprised at what I can do. Launch night, you will know everything."

"There will not be a launch, you have bought the building. You said you were representing a family."

"Of investors. It's not usually what I do, but they asked me to do them a favour and I obliged." The door opened and dinner was served. The food was delicious and Dominic kept filling her glass up. Lia refused the last glass and she asked the waiter for a pot of tea. Dominic was watching her. Lia declined a dessert, she just drank another cup of tea. Suddenly, she wanted to know why he never trusted her, where that came from she had no idea, but she needed to ask him.

"You don't trust me, do you, Dominic Delgado, that's why you had the small lounge made into an office and all the security on the penthouse and you have a complete security folder on me, why I want to know." She saw his face change and he was angry.

"How do you know about the folder, Lia, and just so you know, I have every right to know exactly who is on the premises and all about them. Besides, the files on the people on this project are locked in my safe, only I have access to them." Lia stood up and put her coat on. She turned and looked at him.

"That statement does not ring true, if it was, then how would I not know you have a folder on me? I will finish this project as I have given my word, but if you or any of your associates come near me or my family again, I will stop immediately, and I will let the business world know just how you behave." Dominic gets up and gets to the door before Lia.

"Don't threaten me, Lia, you have no chance. I will see you on Monday when the furniture arrives, that's a promise." She walks out to reception. Jim comes in to escort her to the car. Lia declines and waits for a cab and goes home. She walks in and Nancy and Donna are in the lounge drinking wine.

"Lia, you're early, you okay?"

"I could do with a drink." Nancy gets a glass and Donna pours her out a glass of red wine.

"Tell us what happened."

"It was very frosty in the car after what you said to him he was not happy with. Apparently, he bought the whole block, and there will be a launch; the family he represents is a family of investors, and on launch night, I will know it all. I told him I thought he did not trust me hence the office and the top security in the penthouse he never denied it. I told him I would leave if he or his associates did not leave me and my family alone; he said he would see me Monday when the first of the furniture arrives. It looks like he will be breathing down my neck till the project is completed."

"Lia, I'm so sorry, but this, I'm afraid, is turning into a nightmare and it's my fault."

"Mum, I can handle Dominic Delgado because he wants me."

"Lia, that's not funny saying that."

"Mum, it's true, but he will not make a move on me because I'm working for him, he has rules."

"And after, Lia, what then?"

"I will tell him how much I hate him and walk away; he loses." She left her wine and went up to bed with tears in her eyes and her emotions in tatters. All day Sunday, she relaxed in the garden sunbathing and reading a romantic book; she ate

55

breakfast and lunch, but she had a light dinner; she told Nancy and her mum she was getting to work early so everything was ready when the furniture arrived. Lia let herself in through the side gate and up into her office. She switched the lights on and Gregory got a hit on the security panel; he went to investigate and opened the office door. Lia looked up.

"Sorry, ma'am, I was investigating a blip on my security screen; you're very early." She looked at his name badge.

"Gregory, fancy a coffee?"

"I would love to, ma'am, but I'm on duty, I need to get back." He walked out, shut the door and went back to his post. Lia finished her coffee and went over to the building. Gregory was watching her as she entered the main entrance; the security camera picked her up; it was working well. Lia checked every apartment, made sure the covers were on the floors to protect them and went up in the penthouse; it was 7.30. She walked in the kitchen and could see some of the tile had been fitted. The bathroom was complete except for the shower; it needed its electrics installed. She had the wallpaper for the master bedroom, a beige background but two black orchids on the raised paper. She got three rolls at 450 pounds for the three. Lia walked out the master bedroom and Dominic was standing there with a cup of coffee in his hand. She went to walk past him, she was not having any conversation whatsoever with him after Saturday.

"Good morning, Lia, Gregory tells me you were in very early this morning." Lia never even looked at him, she began walking up the stairs; he put the coffee down and stopped her, but he never touched her.

"Talk to me, Saturday night was a disaster, please, Lia." She looked at her watch.

"If you'll excuse me, I have a furniture delivery to organise." She walked around him and down the stairs and out the door. As she got to the office, the first lorry was arriving then the other two and the drivers got out. July got drinks ready and Lia showed the men where they had to go, and the bedrooms were marked with the apartments they were destined for. The main doors were pinned back and security was on reception; six men plus three drivers were security cleared, and after tea and coffee, they started. Six apartments, twelve bedrooms, they were given permission to use all three lifts by Dominic; it made it a lot easier. Tony and Mark turned up and organised the bedrooms going up, and Lia was on hand; each bed had to be put together, the rest of the furniture was all ready to go. Tony was very impressed with the bedrooms in Apartment 6 when they went in. Apartment 5 was almost finished when they stopped for lunch. Lia took them around to the restaurant and Luigi was ready for them. Two hours each apartment meant with luck they could finish today and get going back up to York so the supervisor told Lia. They were back at one and raring to go. Apartment 4 completed then Apartment 3. It was coming towards 5.30, the men wanted to work on and the drivers were sleeping in the office, so drinks were coming from the restaurant. Two more hours and the last bedroom was in Apartment 2 and the job was complete. They woke the drivers up and Lia thanked them. Suddenly, Dominic came in the office and called the foreman over, they spoke then shook hands; the paperwork was signed, and suddenly they were leaving. He was standing in front of Lia.

"I now know why you warrant your wages, Miss Westlake, the bedrooms are exceptional, don't you think, gentlemen, nothing like a woman's touch." Then Dominic, Tony and Mark walked out the office. Lia watched them walk into the apartment block. Lia turned to July ignoring the man.

"Thank you for your support, July, without you today helping, I would have fell flat on my face."

"It's sure a case of men stick together, but I saw him give the foreman an envelope, Lia, something for the boys I think."

"Let's go home, July, ten in the morning not before I need my bed." Lia got home. Nancy gave her a glass of wine and a spaghetti Bolognese; she sat and enjoyed it. Donna walked in.

"How did it go, Lia?"

"The bedrooms are all in and the men left just after seven; apparently, July saw Delgado give the foreman an envelope she thought for the men; there were six fitters, three drivers that included the foreman. Now for the couches, they will be here on Friday. Twelve leather couches and six long leather stools, twelve coffee tables and they are expensive and each one slightly different."

Delgado went up in the penthouse to the office. As hard as she worked today, he had not changed his mind, he was still going to make her pay.

When Russo Valentino and Dominic Delgado first became business associates in Italy, right from the start, they got on. Each one had a business that complimented each other and it worked. Russo Valentino was shrewd; he was in this late sixties and was branching into the technological world; he had a distribution company and Delgado had the commodities he wanted to distribute; it was a partnership that worked for years until Russo had an accident that meant he could not get around as well anymore so he sold his part of the company to Delgado and he retired to his villa in Milan and conducted the winery from there. Russo had been a very astute businessman; the family had made their own fortunes with their uncle's help; they were millionaires in their own right, but the one thing that made Russo Valentino unique was his duty to mankind; his charities were all to help the poor.

He was talking to Delgado about having an infinity pool installed in the villa bringing the sea into the villa as he could no longer swim in the sea. He put feelers out for someone to design such a pool and he got a lot of response. One such design from a young lady in England which he favoured above every other designs; she was young, vibrant and the pool was unusual. The specialists came in to measure and he gave them the design; they were impressed, and so over nine months, the pool was built overlooking the hillside, a straight line to the sea bringing the sea to the villa, an illusion but when in the pool, all you saw was the pool and the sea; it was spectacular. Russo loved the pool; the water rippled all the time, but as much as he tried to get the young designer out to see the pool, she declined. They spoke often until the sting came. The price for the design of the pool ten thousand pounds and Russo paid without challenging the price and never heard from her again. Russo died five years later not talking to the young woman who designed his pool. Dominic Delgado was going to teach her a lesson she would never forget. Valentino was affected by the fact his vision of the young designer was marred by the fact she gave him her design then went back on her word. Being Italian, your word was your bond and she broke that bond, and as much as Russo loved the pool, what she did marred the pleasure he got from the pool, but he relented and in his will he left her the money because of the pleasure the pool gave him, but he never forgot that she went back on her word, and Dominic was going to make her realise what she actually did to Russo Valentino.

Lia was in early and Judy was with her; they made the beds in the appropriate colours and set the cushions and the rugs; each bedroom finished, even July was helping. The lounges left with the floor protectors until the couches arrived. Lia went up to the penthouse; she pressed in the security number and the door opened, no security to be seen. She walked across the lounge, at least the walls were painted. She went up the stairs to the master bedroom, the paper was up, and Ben was there.

"Come see the walk-in-wardrobe, it turned out well." Lia walked in and the lights came on automatically, and the light interior was very good; the full-length mirror was bigger than she had designed, but it was fine; the shelves were in, the drawers were in, and Ben opened the top drawer and there were small spaces for ties and five other drawers. The metal rails were in and they were in stainless steel.

"I'm putting the bed together tomorrow and the side cabinets."

"Fine, Ben, the leather stool for the bottom of the bed should be here on Friday. I ordered it from York online; it should match with the bedroom." Suddenly, someone was behind her.

"So, Miss Westlake, it's time to go see this company you have been recommended to, we need the Venetian glass. I suggest this afternoon in about an hour; see you in reception." He walked out the bedroom. Ben came up to her, he could see by her face she was upset.

"You okay, you nearly jumped out of your skin as Delgado spoke."

"He made me jump, I never knew he was there." They walked out together. Down the stairs.

"The other two bedrooms will be in by Friday, okay. Monday I will put the treads in for you."

"Thanks, Ben, the bedroom is beautiful." She went out the door to the lift. Down in reception, a man walked in,

"Miss Westlake, the office said I would find you here. Kitchen accessories, I have a van full of gear ordered for you, where do you want it?" She opened a door into a room.

"In there, please." He looked, smiled, then the guy and his mate began to bring the boxes in. Lia sat and ticked everything when suddenly the lift door opened and Delgado walked out.

"There you are ready." Suddenly, the men came in with more boxes and took them in the room.

"Kitchen accessories, they are two days early, sorry, I have to make sure everything is here." In twenty minutes, the lot was stored, and Lia signed and they left.

"Look, may be tomorrow, what do you say?" She shook her head.

"Too much on tomorrow; the electricians are here, the showers have to be connected." He flipped his phone up.

"Tony, you and Mark need to be here tomorrow, the electricians are here connecting everything; you want your money, you do some work." He smiled at Lia.

"Have you had lunch?" She shook her head; he touched her mouth with his finger.

"Lips are made for talking with, use them."

"Sorry, July and I are going for a burger and chips when I have processed this invoice with her help." She walked off, and she saw him get in his car and drive away. She walked up the stairs.

"What did macho man want?" Lia looked at her and laughed.

"We were supposed to go to the glass factory, but kitchen accessories arrived and I had to check the invoice." Between them, they checked it off with the original and it was all there.

"It's a good job, the other lorry arrives on Friday, Lia, you had an email come in."

To: Miss Westlake,
Subject: Building Design
From: Mark Webber.
The stone containers for the front of the building will be arriving on Monday and the men will be setting them out. I hope this is convenient. Please confirm.

M. Webber, Director.

Lia emailed him back.

To: Mark Webber
Subject: Building Design.
From: L. Westlake
Monday would be perfect, thank you.
L. Westlake.

Lia phoned Tony.

"You need to get the outdoor cleaners here on Sunday, the stone pots are arriving Monday morning. This is one job I'm not taking on, sorry."

"Trouble Tony, you look annoyed."

"I was taking a few days off now, Lia tells me the stone pots are arriving and the area around the building needs cleaning up; it's not on her list to do."

"We'll get Mark to help?"

"Can't, he is in Spain for five days, has Lia said anything to you, Dominic, about herself?"

"I have a security folder on her, why?"

"Nothing, I was just wondering, that's all."

"Come on, you have me curious now, Tony."

"When Lia first applied for a job with us, she was just out of university. Her CV was the best Mark and I had ever seen; she passed every exam with A's across the board: design and technology, painting photography, sculpture; she read every book on design through the ages and passed every exam. We needed her, Dominic, she was our ultra-modern designer. Victorian splendour as she called it was fine, but in the 21st century, the people we deal with wanted what Lia had envisioned where design was concerned. Almost seven years, we have had her working for us and now we are going to lose her after this project is finished. Mark seems not that bothered, he seems to think someone else will come along, he is wrong."

"So, did Lia ever diverse into designing anything else other than luxury buildings?"

"She did once, she had been with us a few months we saw an advert in a newspaper for someone to design an infinity pool, you know, one that goes on forever or looks like it does. We had a bet with her that she could not design one and she did and sent the design off to a person in Italy. It was months before she got the letter telling her that her design the said person was going with and she spoke with the man quite often, and apparently, it was built to her specifications."

"Did she ever see the pool up and running?"

"No, she had a very big job on that took a year to complete, a tower block that was converted into luxury flats and she completed it. Mark took over, but the design of the pool was Lia's; nothing to do with us."

"So, you're telling me she designed an infinity pool and she never sold her design to whoever wanted to use her design, are you sure about that? It would have been worth a fortune, surely."

"I have no idea, ask Lia, Dominic, or Mark when he comes home."

"No, actually I prefer this conversation goes no further than this room." Dominic decides to do better than ask Mark; he gets on to the bank and they go back in their records. He will wait for the outcome. He never doubted Russo's story, but before he confronted her, he needed to investigate.

Lia is in the kitchen in Apartment 1. July and Lia bring a trolley up with boxes on it and they start setting out the kitchen equipment. The cutlery is Sheffield stainless steel, the plates beautifully crafted glass and the cup and saucers and small plates the same. All the other goods are in a dark red to match the floor tiles. It's coming together. July and Lia do Apartment 2 same, but the kettle toaster and microwave is in navy blue matching the tiles. Number three is in orange and number four is a beautiful green colour. Five is white and six in lemon. It's late gone seven and they leave. The boxes go in the skip; it's being taken away in the morning. Lia locked up and walks to her car when he passes her.

"Late night again, Lia, you will have to pay yourself overtime."

"By the way, Mr Delgado, I meant to ask you when this project is finished my contract says I get two million pounds bonus. I need to know who will be paying me." He came up to her, she could see he was angry.

"You, Miss Westlake, will get everything you are entitled to trust me my word is my bond." He walked to the car and drove away. Lia shuddered what he said sounded more like a threat, than answering her question. She decided to phone Tony.

"Lia, what can I do for you?"

"Look, I know you have sold the whole project to Mr Delgado, but I want to know who will pay me the bonus that my contract states, Tony, you or Delgado? The conversation I had with him just now when I asked was more like a threat. I'm thinking I may need to see a lawyer, right, Tony, and may be cancel the rest of the project."

"Look, if it makes you happy, I will wire you the bonus, Lia, there is no way Delgado would be paying you, the agreement was with us and we will pay you for seeing to the penthouse." Lia went home. She sat in the kitchen with her laptop on. She checked her account and there was three million pounds in her account. Her mum came in and looked.

"Wow, the job finished, Lia?"

"No, Mum, but Tony came through with my bonus so I have to trust him." By banker's order, Lia put the money in her mother's account for safe keeping just in case. The next day when July came in, her wages had gone up.

"Yes, I did the wages, you have been paid all the overtime you have spent helping me; they have to pay you, July."

"Well, that's a first. Mark does the wages, I never get any extra."

"Have you ever confronted him about it, July?"

"I did a few years ago, he said it was a standard wage nothing extra."

"Well, I suggest you put the extra in another account until this project is finished you are on overtime if it's deemed necessary." Judy phoned.

"Did you suggest I take Mr Delgado to the glass factory, only he has just phoned me and asked me to take him there."

"Judy, be my guest, but please I need some tall long stem vases for long stem flowers; the rest it up to him."

"So, fancy a spot of lunch and I know just where to go."

They ended up by the London eye and a burger restaurant, huge burgers, fries and creamy milkshakes and the rest of the afternoon off.

They finally went back to the office; his car was there, but July and Lia locked up and went. Saturday morning, the skip went and the cleaners were in. Tony was not very happy, it took all day to clean the site up and he needed to be back. Sunday, the lorry would be here with a small crane. Her phone went.

"Lia, how do you want these flower boxes, you do know how heavy they are? They need a small crane to offload them."

"Look at the design and follow it, Tony, it's easy when you know how."

"I can't, it's locked in your office." She sat there so angry. The next day she turned up, at least it was clean. The lorry turned up with the tiny crane on the back; she measured the path by the wall and put a cross, and suddenly, the flower boxes were going down where she wanted them; the men filled the boxes with compost and the small fir trees and plants were encased in the boxes. Suddenly, it changed the whole look of the building, and Lia left Tony to it and went home. She was in the garden sitting drinking tea when her phone went. It was Delgado; she was now recognising his phone number.

"Mr Delgado, it's my day off, what can I do for you?"

"Who the hell said you could put boxes of plants outside my building?"

"I did, it's part of the design we agreed."

"Not with me, you never."

"Well, seeing you were a late arrival, it was already set in stone. By the way, the flower boxes are made of stone you need a crane to get rid of them, good luck." She turned her phone off. Her mum and Nancy laughed.

"Insufferable man. I would so love to throttle him. Nancy, if he comes here, I have moved to Siberia, right."

"Yes, Lia, Siberia isn't that near Russia and it's freezing so I believe." They both laughed. Lia never got a ring back. The next morning, the lorries arrived with the couches and the long leather stools; and the cleaners were in hoovering the floors, and two couches and two antique coffee tables were put in each apartment; the stools were for the bottom of the beds; the apartments were almost complete. A van drew up with all the glass Lia bought and that all went in the small room by the reception. Lia did a walkthrough with Judy and July. The cushions were put on the beds and the couches. Six apartments completed but for the glass Lia bought and the flower arrangements to be completed. The reception area was cleared and the computers installed. Ben took the rest of the week and the bedrooms were complete, and Lia and July made the beds, the treads were in and the stairs covered again. Two days later, the couches arrived and the coffee table arrived; it was exquisite. When Lia came in, a painting was in the centre of the room, and it was Claude Monet's *Water Lilies*; she stood looking at it.

"You like it, Lia?" She turned and looked at Dominic.

"More than I like you. He was an artist that knew what he wanted to paint. He hated people discussing his painting, you either love it, or hated it that's what I like about Claude Monet, an uncomplicated man whose paintings were for the twentieth century." She walked away.

"Is the penthouse nearly done? I was going to have the launch next Tuesday if that's okay with you."

"Fine, Tuesday it is. I will order the flowers, or do you not want flowers?"

"Lia, you can have what you like."

"Really not possible. I would end up in prison." She was gone. The glass was put in the apartments and Lia would with July fill them with flower displays; this was the fun bit. Monday morning, the flowers arrived, and Judy arrived with the cushions for the penthouse. She came back to the apartments.

"Have you seen the penthouse? The beautiful glass Dominic bought has flowers in them and they are awful." They go up in the penthouse and they can hear raised voices before they open the door.

"Dominic, you would not let me do anything, do you not like the flowers I picked?"

"Elena, I do not want you interfering, please go, this is nothing to do with you. The penthouse is Miss Westlake's domain."

"Taken her to bed, have you, Dominic? Took your vengeance out on her? I hope you have for what she did to Russo Valentino; she is a thief and you know it. Since the will was disclosed, you have been on a mission to get her. You need to teach her a lesson. Russo Valentino spoke highly of her yet she actually broke his heart." Lia looked around, shook her head and walked back to the lift; they followed. Down in reception, they went in the back room.

"What the hell was that all about, Lia, whose heart did you break?" She sat down. July gave her tea; they had coffee.

"I have been left a million pounds in Russo Valentino's will and I broke his heart, I don't get it. Let's get on with the flowers, but please stay with me." She was shaking, she loved Russo Valentino although she never ever saw him and she had no idea what she did to him, and she was not a thief. Judy and July began with Lia to make the displays up. All too soon, they were finished and they cleared the stalks and paper away. The flowers looked awesome.

"The penthouse, Lia, we're going to try and salvage the flowers."

"No, let it stay as it is, we're going home, he can get a florist in to put it right." July and Judy left. Lia gave them both invites to the launch. They both wondered what the conversation they heard was all about. She sat and drank a cup of tea, then washed her cup up and left. She got to the office, unlocked and walked in. This had been hers for two years since the building started. She got a box and took her books and her designs; they were hers, she was not leaving them behind; she would start again somewhere else. She put them all in the boot of her car and drove out the complex for the last time. When she got home, Nancy thought she was very quiet, but she ate dinner and drank a glass of wine.

The launch was at 7.30 and Lia paid for Nancy and her mum to have a complete makeover. The salon was waiting for them. Lia packed and put her case in the boot of the car. They were all dressed and ready to go at 6.30, and the cab arrived. Judy and July were waiting for Nancy, Lia and her mum when they got there. The reception was heaving with people. Tony came up to them.

"Lia, people want a tour of the apartments, are you going to show people around? Mark is showing two couples Apartment 6, but he is out of his depth." Suddenly, she is being taken in the lift; she looks up, its him.

"You owe me. I had florists here all morning doing flower displays, you did not do a good job, Miss Westlake." The door opened and the people in the room were few but mostly Italian.

"Ladies and gentleman, at last you meet Miss Lia Westlake, the lady responsible for not only the penthouse but the six apartments below the penthouse." A woman came up to her.

"You are so clever I wish I had your talent. My house in Florence could do with a makeover, would you consider it?"

"Maybe, but I need a holiday before I take on any more work, this project has taken two years out of my life." Dominic came up to her.

"Hanna, would you excuse us, we need to talk, we will be back, enjoy yourselves. There is food in the kitchen, could you organise it for me? I would be so grateful." He led her through the corridor; she knew where she was going, his office. He locked the door.

"Sit down, Lia, I have something to give you." He opened the draw and gave her an envelope. He left it on the table by her.

"Your inheritance from Russo Valentino, who I may say adored you even though he never actually met you, he spoke a lot about how a young lady designed him an infinity pool out of the goodness of her heart and he had it implemented and enjoyed swimming in it. Although the sea was at least thirty minutes by car away, you designed it so it seemed the sea was part of the pool, and it is exceptional." Lia had tears remembering the conversations they had had; she never knew her dad, he died a few weeks after she was born. Russo helped her; she told him her story. Nine months off and on, they spoke then it ceased and Lia got on with her life. He leaned on his desk.

"Why the hell did you demand ten thousand pounds for the design of the pool a year after you stopped talking to him?" Lia looked at him and shook her head. There were tears, but she stood up. She pushed the envelope towards him.

"One, my designs are mine, if I design something, it's mine. I never sell my designs. I may implement them like the design in this penthouse, but the design stays mine and it can never be repeated. I was twenty-one, just got a job with Grossman and Partners, I was about to start my first job when Tony gave me a project to do, an infinity pool, and I did. I studied what an infinity pool was and designed it and sent it to Mr Valentino. I never expected to hear from him. It was months before I did and not at work. I was flattered and we talked, and he had the pool built and that was that. I never sold my design to him; it's not what I do."

"I don't believe you. Russo sent you a cheque for ten thousand pounds, Lia, and it upset him so much, not that he could not afford it, but because you told him it was gift from you to him; he fell in love with you Lia; talking to you made his day." She stood up and walked to the door.

"Take the envelope, Lia, take your pound of flesh now before I do something I will regret." She stood with her back to him by the door and folded her arms.

He came up to her, turned her around and tried to put it in her hand; she refused to take it. Suddenly, there was a knock at the door.

"Lia, are you in there? I have been looking for you." Lia walked to his desk and sat down; he opened the door. July came in.

"Lia, you're needed downstairs, people are asking for you." She stood up, tore the envelope in half and threw it in his face and left the office and went down to the venue. People were viewing the apartments; it was just a smoke screen; she knew he was not selling any of them. Lia smiled and answered questions; her mum was so proud of her. She needed to talk to Mark, but he kept avoiding her. She sat down and suddenly remembered Mark had her design book and it had disappeared. She caught him in the reception area.

"Talk to me, Mark, or I will make a scene. What did you do all those years ago, Mark, tell me for God's sake,"

"Nothing, I did nothing, Lia. I have no idea what you're on about."

"I'm going to have it out with Dominic Delgado. I'm getting to the bottom of this. I don't care who is in the penthouse. I'm not a thief and I'm not a liar. I will run you, Mark."

"You can't. I sold the design to Russo Valentino if that's what this is about, you did it in our time at the office and I had every right to get Russo Valentino to buy the design; he used it to build himself a pool. We would have got nothing out of it, that's what business is all about."

"Have you any idea what you have done, Mark? You have maybe ruined me, for what, ten thousand pounds? Did you send Senior Valentino my design book?" Suddenly, Tony is there and he is angry. Lia turns to him.

"Were you part of this as well, Tony? I trusted you both and you have stabbed me in the back; my reputation is trashed, and Delgado is threatening me."

"Of course, he didn't, Lia. I looked everywhere for that design book, and I took it."

"What did you do with the money, Mark?"

"I put it in your account, it was yours, you had the right to it."

"You're a liar, Mark, there is no way I would not have known ten thousand pounds went into my account."

"Okay, I put it in then took it back; it was in your name. I used it in the business; it was a fair price for your design. It was seven years ago how was I to know this would happen?"

"It meant Delgado had all the evidence after Russo died and he came after me, Mark, and he is a very influential man." Lia walked away.

"This was why he bought the building, Mark. Lia said something was wrong and her instincts were right."

"How was I to know seven years on the old man would die and leave the information in his will?" Lia was standing in turmoil.

"The problem is how do we limit the negative publicity from this, Lia."

"We can't, he has investigated and has found the money went in my account, and then I took it back out according to you. It looks like I was hiding it, and looking at your face, Mark, you're not going to tell the truth. I have already torn a brown envelope he gave me up with one million pounds in it. I'm leaving and I'm going to try to start again but as far away from you as possible. I'm sorry, Tony, you at least have principles, maybe you need a new partner." She walked away. She went over to her mum and took a glass of champagne.

"Maybe she is right, Mark, without Lia we're done for." The lift opened and the man himself walked out; he came over to Tony and Mark.

"I have been looking for you, maybe you would like to come up to the penthouse, there are prospective clients who want a word with you." He came over to Lia and was smiling.

"I was hoping to get your daughter back up in the penthouse, people are asking me questions only she can answer. Would you like to join us, Mrs Westlake Donna?" He escorted them into the lift, and Lia just looked ahead of herself; Donna was chatting to Dominic. The lift opened and the party was really going on, waiters with trays of food and drinks were flowing. Her mum was shocked at the opulence of the place.

"Lia, I knew you were good, but this is spectacular."

"Yes, I think Lia is a genius if I do say so; it's everything I wanted it to be and more." Suddenly, a glass is put in her hand. She sits down, she can see Mark and Tony talking to a man and then they were pointing at Lia. Her mum went off with Dominic up the glass stairs, and Lia walked out the lounge and through the corridor; she got to the small room she never had any input in. She opened the door, it was set out as a library. She looked around and they looked like all first editions; a very expensive room, then she saw it: her design book. She went over and picked it up. She sat on the chair looking through it and tried not to get stressed. The door opened and a woman walked in.

"So, you found it; the book belonged to you; it cost Russo Valentino ten thousand pounds; you sold the design to him a year after the pool was built, why, Miss Westlake, I'm trying to understand ever since the will was read. Dominic confided in me what he found out and he was on a mission to get the answers." Lia put the book back in its place. She went to walk out the door. "No, you're staying here till you tell me, explain to me after being on friendly terms with Russo you did that to him, why? He adored you from afar."

"All I can say is none of it is true, yes, I designed a pool, no, I did not sell my designs to him."

"Really, is that what you're going with?" The woman walked out the door and she locked it so Lia could not get out. She sat there waiting for her to come back. The door opened and she came back in and gave her a folder; it said Lia Westlake.

"I suggest you read the contents then, if I were you, I would change your career; you will never work in the Design and Technology industry again Dominic will see to that. Was the ten thousand pounds worth it, Miss Westlake?"

Lia sat and she looked through the folder, it was a very thorough investigation of her from being young to the end of this job; there were photos and some were quite surprising and where they came from she had no idea, but some was from her university days. She put the folder on the shelf with her design book and walked out of the room. She avoided the lounge and went down the back stairs; she rang her mum; she was going home with Nancy, it was up to her. Nancy and Lia were having a cup of tea when the lift opened and Mr Delgado walked out with her mother; they came over to Lia.

"It's early, darling, and you want to go home you're the star of the show and people wants to talk to you."

"I'm through talking. Nancy and I are leaving, you can stay, it's up to you." Suddenly, the driver walked in.

"Miss Westlake, cab for Miss Westlake." Nancy and her got up.

"So, Dominic, we would love to have you for lunch tomorrow if you can make it." He kissed her hand. Lia walked away. In the cab, her mother told her off; she had no idea what was happening. Back at home, Lia made herself a hot chocolate and went to bed. Her phone went and she picked it up.

"Don't hang up we have a lot to sort out, Miss Westlake, if you don't cooperate, I will ruin your reputation and you know I have the means to do it, so I'm offering you a way out, spend the weekend with me and I will leave you alone, but you're mine from Friday to Sunday night, agreed? At least, I get to punish you for the hurt Russo Valentino went through." She turned her phone off; she was not giving herself to him if that was the punishment he was dealing out. The next morning, Lia was gone. She went down to Dover and drove onto a ferry leaving her phone locked in the drawer in her bedroom. She had taken one million pounds out of her account and left. Dominic was in the penthouse having breakfast, and when he went in his office, he immediately realised the drawer where he kept his files was open and the only file missing was Lia Westlake. He got on to security and Thomas came up. They did a scan of the penthouse and found the folder in the library next to her design book. The contents were all there; he was wondering how it got there. He phoned her and it went to voicemail. He sat and looked through the design book; it was exceptional; she was exceptional, and the weekend was the one thing he was looking forward to.

Tony was seriously thinking, the inquiries they got last night were coming to nothing. Lia would never work for them again. He rang her and it went to voicemail. He rang July, she told him she had phoned her and it went to voicemail. Nancy took Lia up some tea; she walked into her bedroom.

"Donna, seen Lia this morning?"

"No, I have a headache on top of a headache. I thought she was still in bed." Nancy rang her, she heard the phone and opened the drawer to see Lia had left her phone behind.

Nancy came back up, the car was gone and a lot of her clothes were gone. Donna began to cry.

"Where is she, Nancy? I know the last few months have been stressful, but last night, she seemed fine." July and Judy came around after Donna phoned them. July phoned Tony and he was shocked; now they were in trouble and Mark was whinging about the money they were going to lose if they didn't find her. July and Judy were phoning around to try and find her. Her phone went and July picked up, she knew immediately it was the man himself. She needed to make an excuse.

"Mr Delgado, I'm afraid, Lia is not here at the moment. I will get her to call you as soon as she comes in." July turned her phone off. Donna was out of her mind with worry; she had been gone only a few hours. Lia got off the ferry and drove to Paris; she was staying the night, in fact she stayed a week. Lia got herself a road map and began to plan her journey. She was free and was not thinking about anything but herself for once in her life. Italy, she was heading to Italy; she had a plan. She was eventually aiming for Pisa, she always wanted to see the Leaning Tower. Lia bought herself a decent camera and was having a very long holiday. It took Lia a week to get to Lyon; she stopped at several hotels trying to sort her mind out where she wanted to go, but Lia drove through France stopping and being a tourist wherever she wanted to; she had been gone a month and finally drove into Italy and decided to rest for a while. Lia stayed in Turin for a week and loved the photos she took. Lia decided to drive to Genoa, it was on the coast. She was near to Pisa, her goal, six weeks since she left home. When she got to Pisa, she decided to stay for a while. She was loving the freedom and decided when she would spend the million she would think of going home. She had not made a dent in the money. Security tried to find her but came up with nothing. Dominic phoned her mother several times but got nowhere. Dominic closed the penthouse down; he had lost her and he felt like a fool; he still wanted her but not to punish her; he really missed her and it surprised him. Someone once had told him hatred is on par with love, but he was sure love was an emotion; he only ever felt for his mother.

Dominic decided to visit Lia's mother Donna before he went back to Italy, and he apologised to her. He promised her if he ever found Lia, he would bring her home. Donna told him she wished he had never met her daughter. He left their home after her mother told him things he never wanted to hear.

Lia loved Pisa; she decided to stay for a while so she rented an apartment and began to make friends.

Florence Duvall worked in a restaurant and Lia went in for lunch over there. She got talking to them and got invited to an open theatre that was playing in the town. Lia decided to meet her there. Florence was with a crowd of friends, and two of the boys got a jug of wine and they offered Lia a glass; it was fun. The play was in Italian, but Lia managed to follow the story.

Florence introduced her to Emile, he worked in a company that designed motifs for a T-shirt company, and it fascinated Lia. They met after Emile finished work and they had coffee together. Lia gave him a few ideas she had and he thought they were great; she told him he could use them she just wanted to keep her hand in. They were sitting by the sea front.

"So, what are you running away from, Lia?" She looked up at Emile.

"What makes you think I'm running from anything?"

"You're not the typical tourist and you said you have been touring through France and now you're in Pisa, where next, Lia?" She looked up at him; he could see tears. He put his arm around and cuddled her.

"Could you not tell me what's bothering you because something is. I promise your secret is safe with me." She smiled and kissed him on the cheek.

"It happened too long ago to be resolved, besides a certain person did a job on me and no one can put it right. He was my boss and he stole my design and sold it to someone I was fond of, and when he died, in his will he left me money that I could not accept, but he left an account of how I hurt him, and it was my boss not me. If I try going back, the person who has the so-called evidence will ruin my reputation, so I'm trying to find myself. It's hard, Emile. I love designing and I have designed some very iconic apartments in the seven years I have been doing it, now it's all gone, and I'm lost."

"Can you not design under another name, Lia?"

"No, he offered me a way out: spend a weekend with him and he would leave me alone. I can't sell myself for a career, so I did the only thing I could: I walked away." Emile cuddled her, and for the first time, she sobbed in his arms. A few days later, Lia said goodbye to the crowd and in particular, Emile and she was back on the road. This time, she went to Florence; she needed to explore on foot, no cars allowed. She decided on a hotel and signed in as Lia Westlake. Suddenly, Dominic Delgado got a phone call, a women answering the name the hotels were to look out for was actually staying in his hotel in Florence. That afternoon after face recognition came through, it was Lia. She had been found after eight weeks, and he needed to approach her gently. He came to the hotel; the manager said she was out exploring the town. Dominic sat watching the door. Lia came back, but she sensed something was wrong. She took her key and went in the lift, came out on her floor and went in the suite. She had a drink then ran a bath.

80

She had taken some beautiful photos and was thinking of taking up photography. She turned the tap off and was going to get undressed when there was a knock on the door; she opened it and he was standing there.

Lia opened her eyes; she was on the bed with a cold cloth on her head, and he was sitting beside her. She scrambled up the bed. Dominic stood up and moved away.

"Calm down, I'm not going to do anything, Lia, everyone has been so worried about you, me included." She just looked at him.

"I bet you were; you missed your weekend with me not that I was ever going to let you touch me. Get out of my room. I'm paid up to the end of the week." He moved away from the bed and stood by the window.

"Ring your mum, Lia, she is in pieces. You were wrong to leave without talking to her. Tony and Mark are struggling; the business is fading without you there."

"You stand there talking about the business when you must know what was done to Russo Valentino was nothing to do with me; it make me sick to think about Russo Valentino dying thinking I was not who he thought I was, and I can never make it right, so it's good, serves Mark right, he made all this happen, and I will never work for them as a designer again. I hope the company goes down the tubes. I will never design another building ever." He sat on the bed but not too close.

"It's in your blood, Lia, designing, and you know it." She got off the bed and stood looking out the window.

"I need you to go now, please. I will leave in the morning. I can't stay here now. I need to move on." He was behind her; he never touched her but kissed her cheek.

"Don't run, stay for a while. I will leave you alone, the suite is yours for as long as you want it." He walked to the door; she turned.

"Tell me, Dominic, if I had defied you and stayed and ignored your threats, would you have destroyed my career? I need to know." He turned and looked at her.

"Yes, then I would have. I was beyond angry with you. I actually wanted to strangle you, you have no idea, but now, no, I think I would have thought it through better." He shut the door; she had her bath, and that night, she was too distressed to eat and went to bed. They reported to Mr Delgado that the lady in question was down eating breakfast and she was going out; she had her camera with her. Donna and Nancy were at the airport, and Dominic took them to the hotel. He had them in the penthouse. Lia came into the hotel and she got in the lift, but it bypassed her floor and opened on the top floor. She stood there and suddenly her mum was standing there. She came towards Lia and she was suddenly in her arms. They were both crying. Nancy came out and took them both in. Donna sat Lia down and Nancy gave her tea.

"He brought you here, didn't he, Mum? Tell me."

"He said he would find you if he could and reunite us again. God, Lia, I have been so worried, you should have phoned at least. I could not phone you, come home, please."

"No, what's the use? My career is finished, so I'm staying in Italy for a while then I'm going to Spain, and maybe I will find something I want to do, sorry, I'm staying in Europe. England has lost its charm, Mum, sorry."

"Lia, nobody is going to stop you for doing what you do best: designing."

"Only me, Mum. I can't prove I never did what he accused me of doing because the man who died thought I was dishonest and that can never change. No, I'm never designing ever. I need to go down and shower. I'm hot and I have a headache." Donna cried after she left.

"Nancy, this will never get better. I'm losing my daughter because of a lie and there is not a damn thing I can do about it." Lia showered and dried her hair. She laid on the bed wrapped in a robe and drifted off to sleep. She dreamed she was in the penthouse and he had locked her in the library. Lia woke up in a sweat; she needed a drink. She sat on the veranda drinking a bottle of water. She sat looking over the city; there was a lot she needed to see; she would not be coming back this way again. It made her sad, she hated living out of a suitcase. She finally came down to the restaurant and needed a table for one, and the waiter took her across to a table by the window. Suddenly, Mr Delgado was standing by the table.

"The least you can do is join us for dinner; your mum is anxious to see you."

"I spoke to her, I'm not going back. I have decided to stay in Italy for the time being." He leaned in and helped her up.

"Then you won't mind having dinner with her before she goes home." He walked her across to a table where her mum, Nancy and a woman were sitting, she was Italian. Dominic sat Lia by her mum. He sat down and the waiter brought up bottles of wine. Lia refused wine, she asked for a fizzy water with ice and the waiter brought it back.

"A little wine would not hurt you, Lia."

"I don't drink, Mum, I find alcohol messes with my brain. I prefer to be sober more at this very moment." She looked across at Dominic, she could tell he was angry.

"Dominic, you have not introduced us, that's not like you."

"Celeste, this is the woman you wanted me to introduce you to. Lia Westlake, she designed the building I currently own."

"My dear, the penthouse is to die for, wherever do you get your inspiration from? I have a chateau, and although beautiful, I want it re-modernised but also keep a lot of the original features, would you be interested?"

"No, I do not design anymore. I decided I'm going into photography, it's less time consuming and a great deal more fun. When I finally get back to England, I'm going to open a small shop and sell framed iconic places of interest around Europe."

"Dominic, please make her change her mind." Dominic smiled.

"Celeste, Lia designed your pool when she was twenty-one, I do believe." Suddenly, Lia was feeling sick and her mother saw Lia's face change, but before her mother could get to her, the woman spoke.

"You designed Russo's infinity pool, wow, it's beautiful, you must be very clever." Suddenly, Lia got up, the glass went over spilling the contents on the table. She walked away while Dominic got up.

"I will go, Donna, I need to put this right." Lia walked out the hotel over to the beach and sat down; this nightmare was never going to end. He sat down near her.

"I'm sorry that was unforgivable, but I wanted to demonstrate that there are only a few people who know about Russo Valentino and the pool and less even about the contents of his will." She looked at him.

"You know and that's enough for me and the woman who locked me in your library and came back with the folder you had on me. Tell me when I first saw you in that hotel, did you know who I was?" He sat closer to her.

"Yes, and I was surprised it was you, but you were so focused on what you were doing at the time."

"I'm sorry I never thought someone could go to the lengths you have gone to. I need you to leave me alone. I can't change what happened, but I can change myself, and I will."

"You know my opinion, Lia, on the subject, and it has not changed, but you could make up for what happened. Go to the chateau, make it modern, make Russo Valentino's chateau a masterpiece. You have as much money as you could possibly need and you can change almost everything you want to; the possibilities are endless; it's an opportunity you will never get again, think about it, make up for what you did to Russo." He stood up.

"Please come, dinner is being served."

"You go, I'm not hungry, food does not bother me, sorry." Domino got up and walked back across the road into the hotel. Donna was upset, but the dinner went ahead. They left the lounge at 11.30. Lia never came back in for dinner. The next morning, Donna was informed she had gone, but she left a letter for her mum with the reception.

Dear Mum,

I'm sorry, but I had to go. I'm getting there and I will be home but not just yet. I will never work for Tony and especially Mark, he was the one who sold my design to Russo Valentino, but I can never prove it because he put the ten thousand pounds in my account then took it out again and put

it into the business. Tony knows, but he too has his hands tied.
I have never sold my design books, Mum, I have them all,
except the infinity pool design. Dominic Delgado has it in his
library in the penthouse, that's how this all started and now
it's ruined my career. Seeing you brought it all back again,
but I know I can't run forever, but I will phone you, promise.
I know I'm telling the truth, but every time I think of Russo
Valentino, my heart is breaking for that man I loved. Mum,
we spoke so much and what Mark did can never be undone,
but I can't live with people thinking badly of me, so I'm going
away, and I'm sorry I will never set foot in England again.
Lia Westgate is me, but at the moment, I wish she was not me.
I'm sorry, Mum. I love you.

Lia.

Donna sat down; she had tears in her eyes. She was going
back home; she wanted to leave now her daughter had left.
They were in the restaurant having breakfast; Dominic came
up to the table.

"So, by your face, you know Lia has gone, I'm so sorry."
Donna put her folk down, she had had enough of everyone
thinking her daughter was a liar and she was making waves,
big waves and she was getting to the bottom of all of this.

"Tell me, Dominic, do you have Lia's design book in your
library at home in the penthouse?"

"Yes, it was given to me to give back to Miss Westlake
by Russo Valentino, he was very fond of Lia, as well you
know."

"You are a very convincing liar, Mr Delgado. Is that the
way you conduct your business, you set out to ruin my

daughter's reputation, but she left before you could achieve your goal, but you succeeded or Russo Valentino did, the mistake can never be eradicated because he died not knowing the truth, here read the letter Lia left me then I never want to see you ever again." Dominic walked away and read the letter. He took a copy and gave Lia's mother back the original. That morning, they went back on a commercial flight. Donna wanted nothing to do with the Delgado family, she was keeping her fingers crossed Lia would phone her. Delgado got on to his security, he wanted a money trail investigated. The cheque was made out to Lia Westlake and it was issued by Russo Valentino in 2007 and he wanted to know where it was cashed and who got the money. Meantime, he got on to his security in Italy and he wanted her found. Lia decided Rome was her next stop, not a lot of distance from her enemy as she was now calling him, but she decided to stop off at Perugia, a hillside city, very much the essence of what Italy should be. Lia was excited here, she could let her design imagination run away with her; she was excited for the first time in weeks. She parked up and walked into the hostel called Little Italy. She signed in as Lia Judy and the proprietor showed her into the room with a private bathroom. Lia stripped off and had a shower then she dressed in trousers, a shirt, a hat, glasses and her camera, money in the pocket, and she went out.

"Miss, if you walk to the tram station, you can get up to the hillside city."

"Thank you, I will do that." Lia got on the cable car, it creaked and stopped and started, but eventually, they got there and she was in what looked like a medieval city. To Lia, it was beautiful; she sat at a cafeteria and had a big pizza, a salad and a glass of tea. Lia took so many photos then she donned a scarf on her head and went in the Cathedral of Lorenza. The medieval art on the walls gave Lia such a thrill; photos were not allowed, but she bought a book on the art. Lia was out most of the day and she was hungry again so she came back and sat at a restaurant and had a huge meal of meat, local vegetables and a dessert with a glass of wine. Lia walked in the hostel. She went up to her room, showered and sat looking through the photos she took; some were to dark, so she deleted them but a lot she was pleased with. The next day, she decided she was heading for Rome. Dominic was in his office; there was no let-up in him, he was more focused than usual. She had been gone a week and she was off the horizon; he was getting more angry each day that passed and she had not been seen.

He decided to go to England, he needed answers. The jet landed at Heathrow Private Jet Service and he was on his way to the Savoy Hotel, one of the penthouse suites were available and a list of requirements were adhered to. Tony was in the office, the company was not doing well, they had offers of work but two clients wanted their services, and when the potential clients were told Miss Westlake was not available, they declined an alternative designer. Tony was drinking a coffee and Mark was out showing a client an apartment that had come on their books. The door opened and Liz came in.

"Tony, a Mr Delgado is in the outer office, he wants a word with Mark."

"Show him in, Liz, he is one of our clients or was. I will see him bring a tray of coffee in, please." The door opened and Tony came over to Dominic and shook hands with him.

"I'm afraid, we have had no communication from Lia in weeks."

"That's is why I'm here. I have seen her and so has Lia's mother; we found her in Florence, she registered in one of my hotels, so I took her mother out to see if she could persuade her to come home."

"So, Lia is back, thank God, we need her, the clients only want Lia designing for them; it's getting ridiculous."

"No, Lia is not back and now I know the truth. I came here because Lia needs to stop running." Tony just looked at Delgado.

"You are one of the reasons Lia is running. I'm the instigator, but now I know the truth and so do you. Lia designed a pool for a dare from you, Tony, when she first came to work for you and she did it and she sent her design to the man in Italy, Russo Valentino, you remember I see by the look on your face. He died six months ago and I was the one commissioned to implement his will that's when the story came to light. The infinity pool is everything Lia designed and Russo spent many times swimming in it, but he kept a secret, the young girl whom he adored demanded ten thousand pounds from Russo for implementing her design, and by paying the money by cheque, he was sent the design book which he kept. Russo Valentino when he died left instructions with his will, it said I was to give Lia Westlake one million pounds and her design book back. I was going to do that, but trust me, I was also going to ruin her career like she ruined Russo Valentino's faith in human nature. I almost did, but before I could implement what I was going to do, she left, Tony, and trust me, Lia is never coming back." Liz came in with a tray and poured out a coffee for both men and left.

"Did you get to talk to Lia at all?"

"Yes, she told me to get out of her suite in the hotel. I told her she had the suite as long as she wanted it, but the next morning, she was gone, but here's the reason I'm here, Lia left her mum a letter and she let me read it, and trust me, someone is taking responsibility for what they did to Lia, and you know who it was, because she said your hands were tied. So, you knew Mark sent the design book to Russo after he deposited the cheque in Lia's name, then when it cleared, he took it back out and used it in the business. I need you to tell me the truth, Tony, what the hell happened?" Tony knew the game was up, but he was not taking the responsibility for what Mark did, but he had no idea what Mark did until Mr Delgado bought the penthouse outright and then a few conversations he heard that mentioned the infinity pool.

"Look, Lia had just been employed by us, we had no idea what Lia could do, and after she designed the infinity pool, she began to design a whole tower block for us, and you know yourself, how good she was. Mark was very focused on the business, and when the design for the pool was chosen, he went into business mode, and as Lia designed the pool while working for us he decided a fee was due from Russo Valentino, and Mark said he was glad to pay. Look, I know nothing about the money side of it. I only know he got the fee and Lia could not find her design book. I tried talking to Mark, he refused to talk about it." Suddenly, the door opened and Mark walked in.

"Mr Delgado, nothing wrong with the apartments or the penthouse I hope."

"Mark, Mr Delgado is here because he has spoken to Lia and so has her mum. Lia left her mother a letter and Mr

Delgado has a copy of the letter." Mark just looked at Mr Delgado, he didn't seem to care.

"The letter states that you sold the design to Mr Valentino and you wanted ten thousand pounds, which you put in a savings account in Lia's name, then you took it out when the cheque cleared, covering your tracks, but the will revealed what happened. The only thing is Russo died believing Lia asked for the money for her design, and in his dying wish, he wanted her to have a share of the pleasure she gave him so he left her a million pounds and he gave her back her design book. I should destroy you, but you have done that yourself, you had no idea that you had a genius in your hands and you lost her, and because of that one mistake, you will lose your business, and I'm actually sorry for Tony, not you." Tony looked at Mark and he just smiled.

"Lia designed the infinity pool while she worked for us, so her design belonged to the business and she had no business giving the man the design for free, and yes, Russo Valentino agreed to pay the ten thousand pounds and I suggested the design book so it was a fair exchange, so try suing me, it was above board."

"Thank you for being truthful and dishonest, and I hope your business fades as it will without Lia."

He walked out of the office; he decided to do nothing, time would tell if they lost the business, but he needed to find Lia. It took Lia two weeks to finish her tour. Rome turned out to be such an iconic city. She threw coins in the fountain, and she rang her mum while she was driving back to France; she was coming home. Lia got to Milan and her car actually died; she needed to buy herself a car. She booked into the Moreno

Hotel and security was alerted. They phoned Dominic, he was on his way back to Italy.

"Sir, we have eyes on Miss Westlake, she is currently residing in the Moreno Hotel, she arrived this morning. Apparently, her car has died on her so she needs to buy a new car."

"I will fly into Milan International, it will take me two hours tops, keep an eye on her, please." Lia had three cases in the suite; she gave the car up, it literally broke down. She had a shower and sent for room service. She ate the English breakfast and needed to sleep; she was so tired as coaxing the car from Rome to Milan had been a nightmare. She closed the curtains and crawled into bed. Dominic got to the hotel and went up in the suite security booked him; he showered and sat on the veranda with a glass of wine; he could see her veranda door was slightly open. Near but still too far apart. He wanted to get her to the chateau; he needed her to see the pool and needed to apologise to her if she would accept his apology. He laid his head back and closed his eyes. Lia was sitting on the recliner watching him sleep, he was handsome that was a fact but scary, and although Lia was calm at the moment, when he would wake up she would be on the offensive again.

"How long are you going to sit there watching me, Lia, how are you?" He sat up, picked his glass up and shuddered.

"I hate warm wine." He got up, pulled the cord around his coat and walked towards the door.

"Would you like a glass of wine, a cold one this time."

"No, thank you, I don't drink wine, but you know that or have you forgotten?" He came out, leaned over and gave her the glass then he picked her up and deposited her on the recliner he was lying on. He gave her back the glass and sat down on the chair.

"A club soda and orange, trust me, it's not alcohol." Lia sipped it, and it was nice.

"I have just come back from England and want to know what I was doing there, Lia?" She just looked at him.

"Okay, I went to see Tony and Mark, things, shall we say, are not going well, they have the clients but they don't have the designer, Lia. I wonder why." She never answered.

"I know the truth, your mother let me read the letter." She put the glass down and walked back to climb over the veranda.

"Mum had no business letting you see my letter, it was personal."

"It was an eye-opener. Tony told me Mark was in business mode when the pool was completed; he got the money in the form of a cheque; he sent your design book to Russo in exchange for ten thousand pounds, and yes, he put it in your account, and after it cleared, he took it back out and used it in the business; he admitted it, he said Russo paid ten thousand pounds for your design book. I'm sorry, God, am I sorry, Lia. I was supposed to give it back to you along with the million pounds." She folded her arms.

"I don't want the money ever." Suddenly, she bent down, she was breathing heavy. He got up and came over to her. She pushed him away and hopped back over, walked in the bedroom and closed the door. Lia drank a whole glass of water; her hands were shaking. She phoned her mum.

"Lia, darling, where are you?"

"Mum, Milan. I was heading home, the car conked out. I have had to get rid of it. I'm in the Moreno Hotel, and

Dominic Delgado is here. I need you please. I want to come home. I've had it with Europe."

"Darling, were on our way. Nancy is coming to stay where you are; we will see you may be tomorrow." She ended the phone call. Donna phoned Dominic; he picked up.

"Lia just phoned me you're both in the same hotel. She is breathless, what's going on Dominic? Her car packed up and she is stranded; we're coming out to fetch her home."

"Don't do anything, I will arrange it, please this might be my only chance."

"Only chance to do what?"

"Put things right between Lia and me. Donna, please let me try."

"Okay, but I'm there when you try. I'm fed up with this scenario." Donna and Nancy packed a case each, and at 4.30, a chauffeur was knocking on the door.

"Ma'am, I'm to take you both to Heathrow Private Terminal, please make sure you have your passports." He smiled. "Boss's orders." They got in the car and arrived at Heathrow Private Terminal. Their cases were taken, and they were escorted into the terminal itself. Luxury was not the word Donna would have used, this was exceptional. They were taken over to a table where suddenly drinks appeared, two glasses of wine and nibbles. A man came up to them, he introduced himself as their pilot; his name was Max.

"Ladies, we will be taking off within the hour; your destination is Milan International Airport, the flight time two and a half hours; dinner is being prepared on board." Suddenly, another man came up.

"Max, your passengers."

"No, Dominic Delgado's guests. I'm the pilot this time, see you soon, ladies." He sat down.

"Business or pleasure, ladies?"

"Neither, my daughter has been touring Europe for ten weeks, we're going out to bring her home, her car conked out and she is stranded in Milan." He checked their passports and wished them luck and then he walked away. Suddenly, an air hostess came up to them.

"Mrs Westlake, if you'll follow me, you can now board the plane." Nancy and Donna walked in, this was more luxurious than the other jet. They sat down, fastened their seat belts and they were taxing down the runway and in the sky. The girl came up to them.

"My name's Jackie and I will be your hostess for the duration of your flight, would you like a drink? Dinner will be served in thirty minutes." They both opted for a cup of tea that was duly brought to them. Back in the hotel, Lia decided she wanted something to eat; her breathing had gone back to normal. She went down in the lift to the restaurant and a waiter came up to her.

"Can I help you, ma'am?" She looked up at him and he smiled; she was beautiful. He could see the suite number on her key tag.

"Table for one, please." He led her over to the window area and sat her down.

"Would you care for a drink?"

"The lady drinks a club soda with lime and plenty of ice. I will have a bottle of Shiraz 98 please, waiter." Dominic sat down.

"At least, have dinner with me, eating alone is boring, don't you think? I promise I will stick to anything you want to talk about even if it's the boring weather." She stayed where she was.

"Mum's on her way. I'm going home, but I'm stuck here, my car gave out on me. I have the money to buy one, but the process is difficult, so Mum will help me back with my three cases of luggage I have, and please, don't volunteer. I don't need your help, just stay away from me, please." He smiled, he had a big hill to climb. He grabbed a chair and sat down.

"So how far did you get, Lia?" The waiter arrived with their drinks and the menu; he gave the tasting to Dominic, he approved, and the waiter poured him a glass.

"You should try this wine, it's sweet and fruity." She began to laugh.

"What did I say?"

"It's not what you said, it's your facial expressions when you said it."

"Maybe it was not the wine, maybe my facial expressions were because I have you having dinner with me." She just looked at him and shook her head.

"The weather has been exceptionally hot the last week." She was telling him to back off, that meant she was bothered with what he was saying. Suddenly, his phone went and he stood up.

"If you'll excuse me, I have to take this. Would you order dinner for us both?" She watched him walk out the restaurant.

"Don, put her on. Donna how was the flight? I'm having dinner with Lia, would you consider going to the chateau and I will bring Lia there tomorrow. Celeste is expecting you both, please don't phone Lia, please trust me, I have her welfare at the heart. What I'm trying to achieve I hope will give her the life back she needs. We will be there tomorrow afternoon."

He ends the phone call and walks back into the restaurant. He can see her giving the menu back to the waiter. He comes up to the table.

"So, you ordered, Lia?" She looked up at him and smiled.

"So, what have you ordered, tell me." He sat down and picked his glass up. She drank her drink and held her glass out.

"May I try your wine but just a little, please?" He pours her half a glass; she sips it and closes her eyes.

"I will order you another drink, Lia." She opens her eyes.

"No, this is lovely, but half a glass will be enough." The waiter came up with their starter, it's lobster. She smiles and looks at his face.

"Yea of little faith, I have seen you eating lobster, and from the look on your face, you loved it." So she has watched him from afar, that's encouraging.

"So, how far did you get, Lia, when you left the hotel?"

"Rome, I got to Rome, stayed a week and decided to go home. I was making my way back to Florence, but the car started playing up long before that I managed to coax it to here and that was it, Betty died on me. I had to scrap her so I came here."

"Betty, you named your car?" She looked up, he was laughing at her.

"I will have you know I named every car I had. Susie was my first at seventeen, then Sissy through university and then Betty, she was brand new when I bought her and I have had her for six years, my fault I ran her into the ground driving around Europe."

"Let me replace her for you, after all, it was my fault I made you run."

"It was a combination of things that made me run not only you." The waiters took the plates and then the main course came up, a paste filled with clams, prawns and chicken. He smiled, no red meat.

"This is delicious, try it, Dominic, you'll like it." He put his folk in and with his spoon tried it, and she was right it was delicious. She was watching his face and suddenly Lia realised she liked what she saw; she actually was enjoying his company. He saw her face change and was hoping she was staying until the end of the meal. She put her folk and spoon down and drank more of the wine; he put some more in her glass and she smiled.

"I'm watching you, Dominic, I'm not used to wine." The waiter took the plates away, and suddenly, the waiter was there with the desserts trolley.

"So, you ordered the meal, my turn to order dessert; it's only fair, Lia." He whispered to the waiter who nodded his head and he dished her up a scoop of fruit then he put on top a layer of pastry then cream then he decorated the plate with strawberries and drizzles of chocolate. He walked off with the trolley. Lia just looked.

"You are joking, if I try to eat all this, I will be sick." He smiled.

"It's to share so are you sitting next to me or me you?" She just looked at him, so he got up and came to join her. He picked up the tiny knife and folk and cut into the pastry, took a small spoon and scooped the dessert up. "Open please." She opened her mouth and he fed her the spoonful, and she ate it looking at him; she thought he was going to kiss her then reality stepped in and she halved the dessert and they both ate out of the same plate. They finished two bottles of wine and

Dominic went back to his seat, ordered tea for Lia and coffee for him. He escorted her to the lounge, but she declined, she wanted to go up. He saw her into the lift and kissed her on the cheek; she blushed but was not looking at him when the lift closed. He needed a drink so he went to the bar. He wanted to take her up, take her to his suite; he wanted her so much. He had another whisky and went up. He sat on the veranda with a coffee; her light was on, but she never came out. He knew he had a lot to overcome with Lia and was thinking about Russo and he knew what Mark did could never be undone, and he knew Lia would maybe not be able to come to terms with the information because Russo died thinking she wanted the money for her design, if only.

The next morning, the waiter knocked on her door; she was invited next door to breakfast; she dressed in a sundress. She knocked next door and Dominic opened it.

"Good, you came. Come in, breakfast is on the veranda, my turn to choose." She walked out and the table was laid up; she sat down. He gave her a bowl of cereals with every fresh fruit you could imagine; she helped herself and he poured her tea. He helped himself; he was eating cereals. She looked up at him and smiled.

"Now what, Lia?"

"I never took you for a cereal man, Dominic." He picked the silver lids up fill with English breakfast. He pointed to the cereals.

"This is the starter, that's the main." She laughed.

"Your mum arrived with Nancy and she wants you to join her. I said I would take you to her. There were no vacancies here, so if you will pack, I will take you to her, say 11 am, okay?" She nodded, but she was not happy, she still never trusted him. She finished her breakfast and hopped over the wall. She showered and dressed in slacks and a pretty top; she had a hat and her sunglasses. The chauffeur took the cases and put them in the boot; she went to pay the bill but reception just took her key and gave her passport to her. He escorted her out to the car, she got in and they were off.

"So, where is my mother, Dominic?"

"Staying in a mansion up in the hills."

"So, you found her somewhere to stay. Yes, she told me she came with Nancy to take you home, you could have asked me, Lia." She never answered him. They started to climb up the hill, and suddenly, Lia recognised the area and she knew where he was taking her. She pressed the button and the chauffeur appeared.

"Please stop the car now, I'm getting out." She undid her seatbelt.

"Tony, stop the car." She opened the door and got out; she walked over to the edge of the road and looked over, there was the sea. He came up behind her; she never turned around.

"What's the matter, Lia?" She turned around; he has never seen her so angry.

"You thought you would fool me? My mother is staying in what was Russo Valentino's chateau, it's not a mansion. I studied the terrane in order to design the pool. I have all this in my memory because you have my design book. I'm going no further. I have no right to be in his chateau, he died thinking the worst of me that I can't change ever, sorry, I'm going to the airport with or without your help." She began to walk down the way they came up. He picked her up in his arms and he put her in the car. He grabbed her hands because she was trying to get out of the car, pulled her in and he kissed her;

shock made her go to punch him. He held her deepening the kiss. He moved his face and she scrambled over to the other side of the seat; she wiped her lips with the back of her hands and the car continued up the hill, through the huge gates and she closed her eyes; he could see tears falling down her face. The car pulled up and her mum climbed in. Dominic got out and Donna had her in her arms and she was sobbing.

"Let's get you inside." She looked at the chateau and thought of the conversations she had had with Russo and shook her head.

"I can't, Mum, he should never have pushed it. I'm going to the airport, can you bring my cases home? I need to go."

"Lia, give us an hour. Nancy and I will come home with you."

"No, I need to do this on my own or I will never get my life back the way I want it. Swim in the pool, Russo loved the pool, it was the last conversation I had had with him." The chauffeur got her cases out and Lia took her hand luggage and her bag and she got back in; her mum watched the car turn around, and she was gone. Dominic came down the stairs, Donna was standing there.

"Where is she, Donna?"

"Gone, Dominic, I'm sorry, she has gone back to England, her cases we're taking them back." He flipped his phone.

"Jerry, where is the jet? Good, get a slot and Miss Lia Westlake is the only passenger back to England, make it happen right, ring me." An hour later, his phone went.

"Thanks, keep an eye on her, tell Jessica." He turned to Donna.

"She is onboard and Jessica my air hostess is looking after her."

He looked at his watch.

"She will be home by 6.30. You can ring her then, Donna or maybe she will ring you." Dominic went up to his office; he got the metal box out of his safe and opened it; everything pertaining to Russo's will was in one place. The only thing missing was the design book which was back in the penthouse. There was a knock on his door and Donna walked in.

"Sit down, Donna, what can I do for you?" She looked at him.

"Are you in love with my daughter, Dominic?" He looked at her and smiled.

"She is adorable, Donna, but no, I'm not in love with her, and up to a few days ago until I confronted Mark and Tony, my opinion was the same, but Mark was the one who sold Lia's design book to Russo for ten thousand pounds; he deposited the cheque in Lia's account and when it cleared put it in the business account, but I was out for vengeance on your daughter and now she will not listen to me; nothing is working." He pushed the box towards her.

"Russo Valentino's paperwork pertaining to his will I had to implement if Lia was not your daughter you would feel the same as I did when I read what Russo wrote. But Lia is right, Russo died keeping a secret for almost seven years thinking Lia lied demanding ten thousand pounds for the design she originally gave him." He got up and left Donna in his office; she took all the papers out, she needed to make sense of the fact he left Lia the design book and a million pounds. She looked through all the legal documents then his bequests to different people's charities; he was a very rich man. Then she came to the heart-breaking letter to Dominic Delgado where he told him about the money he paid for the design book, how shocked he was how they talked twice a week and he told Dominic how confused he was and how the incident knocked his faith in human beings. It made Donna cry, for Russo and Lia. Then she read the paragraph that Russo wrote at the bottom of the letter almost as an afterthought.

"I'm trusting you, Dominic, to make sure Lia gets her design book back; the one thing I know to be true Lia never sells her designs, she implements them, but her design books are hers. I have been following her career and I know this to be true. The million pounds is me saying sorry forgive me for what I know to be true." Donna could not get around the fact Russo was saying sorry to whom. She put the documents back and left his office. They were having dinner when Donna's phone went.

"Lia, you're home, are you okay? Good, now rest, we will be back in a few days with your luggage. Dominic is seeing to it all; it's fine." She handed him the phone; he walked away from the table.

"Miss Westlake, what can I do for you?"

"Thank you for helping me get home, and I'm sorry, Dominic, I know you were trying to help, and as much as it's not my fault, the chateau was Russo's home and I feel I should never step inside his home. Russo died hating me and I can never change that, again, I'm sorry, I hope you can forgive me." The line went dead; he wanted to throw the phone, but he gave it back to her mum.

July came around after she had word Lia was home. Susie came around with her as well; they bought Chinese. Lia opened the door, she was crying in their arms; the girls organised the food and wine, but Lia had tea.

"So, tell us where the hell did you go."

"France to Rome in stages. I have so many photographs I'm thinking of changing jobs, well, starting again, maybe renting a shop and selling framed pictures of iconic places in Europe."

"No, you can't, you need to start your own design company up, Lia, we have had so many enquiries from clients. You do know Tony and Mark are finished; they are splitting up; the business is edging towards disaster. They have the clients, but they want you and your designs and that they can't produce so the clients are going elsewhere."

"Good, I hope Mark goes bankrupt, he deserves everything coming his way; it's Tony I feel sorry for." July and Judy are waiting for an explanation.

"Sorry, still too raw and I'm glad I don't work for Mark anymore." They ate the Chinese, and Lia told them about some of the people she met. They left late; it was like old times and starting her own business was a way to go. She opened her safe and all her design books were there. She decided to go to the office. When she walked in, Cathy was shocked to see her; she phoned Tony who was in and he came down, pulled Lia in and hugged her. He took her up into the office and she sat down.

"How long have you been back?"

"I came in yesterday afternoon from Milan on Mr Delgado's jet."

"So you were with him in Europe?"

"No, I went to Europe to get away from him and all this trouble. I hear the business is failing I'm sorry about that, but I'm never working for Mark again, and if I could prove what he did, I would have him in court."

"Delgado came to see me; he found out what happened, but Mark was very focused and when he sent Russo Valentino your design book, he said you sold it to him." Suddenly, the door opened and Mark walked in.

"So, you're back, Lia, there is a lot of work we can put your way." She stood up.

"I'm taking your clients away from you, Mark. I'm going into business and I'm going to enjoy watching you lose everything. That ten thousand pounds you took off Russo Valentino will be your swan song you're finished." She hugged Tony and left the office. She went back home and decided to ring her mum; she picked up.

"How are you, darling, well rested I hope?"

"Mum, I have decided to start again, it's all I know and I enjoy designing. I'm going to start my own business up in a small way, but I'm going to try."

"Darling, it's your life it's up to you." The door opened and Dominic walked in.

"Darling, I will see you in a few days. I'm glad you're going to work."

"What is she going to do, Donna?"

"Lia is still going to design; she is thinking of starting her own business." He gets back in his office and phones her. She wants to decline his call but answers.

"What can I do for you, Dominic?"

"Let me help please, Lia, I can set you up with a premises to work from and make sure you're okay. By the way, I have got you a new car, you need a car. It's essential, no strings attached, promise." He could hear her breathing hard down the phone.

"Why, Dominic, you do not have to help. I can stand on my own two feet and I will. You believed Russo Valentino and he thought what he was stating in his will was the truth. Mark needs to tell the truth, and unless he does, I want nothing to do with you or the company." She began to look for a premises where she can work and it took a while. July came back to work for her; she was shown a set of offices in the town, a shop that closed down with two floors and it took them two weeks to set it up. The name went up over the top of the window, Westlake Design Company, and it was registered. Her mum had been home a month. Her mum came down with Nancy and they helped. A safe was installed and upstairs was turned into office space for Lia and a kitchen and ladies room.

The downstairs was turned into reception and a luxurious lounge for clients when they opened. Lia got a phone call, Tony wanted to know if she needed help, his business folded, stopped trading, and Mark had gone to America, he was setting up in Los Angeles. Lia phoned her mum, she needed her advice. She phoned Dominic, Lia had not seen him for six weeks, but he said he was around if her mum needed him.

"So Lia has not started designing yet?"

"No, Dominic, she has the office almost complete. Tony phoned, the business folded and he wanted to know if Lia needed any help." It went quiet.

"We know what Mark did, but can Tony be trusted?"

"Lia never had a problem with Tony, and he was a good negotiator; he got a lot of the work for the company."

"Look, leave it with me, I will get back to you then you can tell Lia." Tony got to the penthouse and reception sent him up in the lift; he was surprised Dominic Delgado wanted to see him after the last time in Tony's office.

"Mr Grossman, do come through. I'm glad you made it." The penthouse was exceptional and Tony saw Lia's designs through a different light.

"Lia's mother phoned me, Mr Grossman, she said you are willing to help her daughter, am I right?"

"Lia has set her own company up, I was wondering if I could be of service."

"Why would I let you spoil what Lia is going to achieve, Mr Grossman?"

"Look, even though I was Mark's partner, he was I thought good at what he did, he got a lot of the clients Lia designed for, I was the one that organised everything for the client and Lia. I took a lot of the flack off Lia leaving her to do what she did best, design." He took a list of clients out of his pocket and gave it to Dominic.

"You have a list there of potential clients who wanted our services, the only problem was there was no Lia, she had disappeared."

"So the business failed, you could have taken on new designers."

"No, Mark boasted about Lia all the time, it was wrong, but he pushed her name forward that's why he is in Los Angeles on the back of her name."

"I will tell Lia she can if she wants to employ you. I can't stop her, but just so you know, I will be keeping my security on you." He left the penthouse. Dominic got on to a friend in Los Angeles, he told him a story about Mark James, a new kid on the block from England, he was not to be trusted.

Tony Grossman came on board sourcing clients and Lia took on four students two days a week training. July was loving what she was doing. Six months and Lia was now designing a penthouse in the Canary Wharf area, two flats into a penthouse and it was completely empty. The instruction was to make it exceptional. She had three million pounds to spend. She took the four students with her and they measured up and it meant everything; the penthouse would have five bedrooms a huge lounge, a state of the arts kitchen, dining room, a cinema, gym, the veranda went all the way around the flats; this was going to be a huge job, but Lia was excited. She had six months to do the job after getting planning permission and that was a nightmare to get, but being empty was half the battle. She got home; she already had a theme buzzing around in her brain and the girls threw up ideas even Lia had not thought about. It was Friday night and the surveyors would be there on Monday. Her phone went, she picked up. She froze when she heard his voice.

"Good evening, Lia, how have you been?"

"Dominic, I'm sorry I have a new commission and have as usual thrown myself into it, but we actually start on Monday, what can I do for you?"

"Would you come and have dinner with me, Lia, tonight? I need to talk to you." It went quiet and he waited.

"What do you want to talk to me about, Dominic?"

"No talking over the phone, I need to see your face when I talk to you, besides you owe me a dinner, partner, or have you forgotten?" She shut her eyes; she was shaking.

"I will have dinner with you, where, and at what time?"

"I will pick you up at 7.30 if that's okay with you?"

"Fine, I will see you then." He smiled, he had her he was hoping. Lia was ready and sitting waiting, her phone went.

"Miss Westlake, there is a man down here: Mr Delgado, do I let him up?" She left the door open and he walked in; she turned and was about to smile.

"You're very sure of yourself, Lia, expecting someone, obviously not me, but Dominic Delgado's name got me up here."

"Mark, what are you doing here, you went to America, Los Angeles, I was told."

"Well, I'm back and you owe me. I lost my footing in the American design market, so you're going to pay me what I lost."

"Why should I pay you anything you sold my design book to Russo Valentino for ten thousand pounds and he died thinking I was a liar and went back on my word."

"What word, your designs belonged to the company."

"I had every right to sell it and I want the rest. I have a buyer for them."

"You can go to hell, you're never getting my design books ever." He came towards her.

"Then I will have you, at least I will have something for my trouble." He made a grab for her, and suddenly, he was in a neck hold on the floor. Lia looked Dominic had him. He pressed a number.

"He is in Lia's apartment, come and get him now." Suddenly, the door opened and two men came in, he got him up off the floor.

"You little bitch, one day when you least expect it you will see me, Lia!" Dominic slapped him hard around the mouth.

"It's Miss Westlake to you and you're never going to see her again! Take him away!" Suddenly, they were alone and her legs gave way; he picked her up and sat her on her couch.

"Damn it, Lia, you need something strong and you have no alcohol in the place." He gave her a glass of water. She began to giggle and couldn't stop. He pulled her in and kissed her, and she kissed him back.

"We're going for dinner, remember?" He got her coat, helped her on with it and locked her door and escorted her down in the lift.

"Samuels, Miss Westlake is coming with me; she will be back sometime tomorrow; her apartment is to be secured."

"Yes, sir, done as we speak." He walked her out to the car.

"James, the penthouse please. I have cancelled dinner."

She stops and doesn't get in.

"We're having dinner or I'm going back upstairs."

"We're having dinner in the penthouse and you're staying the night in one of the guest bedrooms, satisfied?" She gets in and they drive off. Lia looks out the window.

"Mark had been followed from the airport, let's say his visit to Los Angeles never materialised as he thought it would."

"I gathered that he had a buyer for my design books."

"I was going to have a word about them to you." She turned looked at him.

"My design books are in the safe; they're just design books."

"Yes, and you have designed some beautiful iconic places with those design books.

"Lia, you need to insure them." She began to laugh.

110

Suddenly, they were there; he showed her to the lift and he pressed his card to the glass and up they went.

"Have you not sold the apartments, Dominic?"

"No, friends and extended family use them when they need to." He took her to the door, it opened and a woman was standing there.

"Good evening, Dominic, where have you been?" He took Lia's coat.

"Lia, meet Chantel, she is here uninvited."

"Come on, Dominic, I have been invited here many times when you needed me. What's her excuse?" He sits Lia down and brings her a glass of white wine; she puts it down.

"Don't I warrant a glass of wine, Dominic?" He ignores her so she takes Lia's and downs it in one go. Suddenly, there is a knock on the door and a woman walks in.

"I'm sorry, Dominic, this will not happen again."

"Rosa, he asked me to come and see him, didn't you, Dominic?" He doesn't answer her.

"She is going home in the morning; she is totally out of control." Suddenly, the woman takes her out of the penthouse, and it's very quiet. He comes back with a fresh glass, this time it's not wine but a club soda with lime. He bends down in front of her and touches her face; she just looks at him.

"What a night, let's have dinner, yes?" He gets on the phone and takes her into the dining room and sits her down. The waiters serve the dinner, but Lia has lost her appetite; she picks at the food and pushes the plate away.

"What if you had not turned up at my apartment, Dominic? This could have turned out very different. I hate feeling vulnerable and now I do."

"He has gone, he is never coming back, that's a promise." He got her up and took her back into the lounge; he put music on.

"Dance with me, Lia." He took her in his arms and pulled her close. He put his arms around her waist and kissed her slowly as he danced with her.

"I have wanted you in my arms like this since I first saw you, Lia, but you were a step too far. I guess Russo Valentino got in the way." She looked at him, leaned in and kissed him.

"I guess, for me he is always going to be there. I wish I had spoken to him before he died, he was the only person I talked to about my feelings. God, he must have hated me! I told him everything; this nightmare is never going to stop." Suddenly, tears were falling down her face. He leaned in and kissed her. She kissed him back.

"I never admit I'm wrong, but this time, God, I wish I at least investigated the letter Russo left me, but I was angry and the design book was with his will, and I went out to destroy you after I got you to work for me. How wrong was Russo and how wrong was I, and now the nightmare is mine because I have fallen in love with you and this problem will always be between us, but I'm willing to try, Lia, so here goes." He picked her up, took her through to his bedroom and laid her on his bed. He took his jacket off, his shoes then her shoes and got on the bed.

"I want to make love to you, Lia, say no and I will stop or I'm going to remove your dress." He unzipped the dress and took it off; she was in lace black panties and a bra. He got off the bed and laid her dress over the back of the chair; he removed his shirt and laid back on the bed.

"So, take off your panties." She suddenly sat up, this was not what she wanted, why did she let him get this far?

"Now you want me to take them off." He leaned in and he unclipped her bra, suddenly her bra straps were sliding down her arms. He took her nipple in his mouth and pinched the other nipple between his fingers.

"Take them off, Lia." She slid the pants down her legs and they were on the floor; he slid his fingers down her body, bent his head.

"You're exquisite, Lia." He began to kiss her, then he went down the bottom of the bed and opened her legs; she began to moan and her body suddenly came alive. He kissed her and kissed her until her body worked through the climax she just had; he looked at her and smiled.

"Say it, Lia, I need to make love to you. I need to feel I'm inside you." He got off the bed and stripped off; she just looked, he was big; she would never be able to take him; he came back on the bed; she just looked at him.

"I need to tell you something please don't freak out." He looked at her.

"You want me to stop, Lia?"

"No, it's just that I have never wanted someone like you until now and I'm scared."

"When did you last have sex, Lia, tell me."

"I have never actually had sex, been near a few times but never wanted to go all the way till now." Dominic got off the bed, put his shorts on and covered her up.

"We need to talk about this, in fact we need to talk about a lot of things." She turned her head away, and he walked out the room. Lia got dressed; she felt such a fool she was going home. The first time she met Dominic, she hated him and he hated her then she realised she loved him, but now wanting to talk about having sex with her was not on. She put her shoes on, she was going home and was not having a conversation with him; she walked to the lift and pressed the button, nothing.

"Where the hell are you going?"

"Home, I'm going home. I may be a fool, but I remember when you wanted me for the weekend and I was to do anything you wanted me to do, if I had agreed, would we still have talked about me being a virgin? There, I have said it." He came up to her and took her back into the penthouse.

"You're staying the night and we're talking whether you like it or not. I nearly took your virginity, Lia, and I could have hurt you, have you any idea how I would have felt if I hurt you?"

"You're hurting me now by talking about it. I want to go, that's three things I need to forget, God, I hate being me." She put her coat on; he came towards her now she was staying and they were talking this through.

"It's okay, I can get a cab." She was walking towards the stairs; she didn't want to cry, she was scared once she started she would not be able to stop. She pushed the door open; he was behind her.

"Stay, I'm sorry, look, I want you, God, how I want you." She turned looked at him and shook her head.

"We are never going to work. I have tried to hate you but I never quite got there, now I have made a fool of myself." He came so close she could feel how turned on he was.

"At least stay the night and I will take you home in the morning, Lia, we have both had a drink." She came back in the lounge and walked up the stairs. He went to follow her.

"I know the way, remember, I designed the place? Good night, Dominic, I'm sorry." He heard her close the door and he drank a large glass of whisky; he went up to bed but stopped at the door where she was sleeping. He opened the door, she came out of the bathroom naked; he just stood there, then walked towards her, leaned in and kissed her.

"Don't please."

"Please what, Lia?" He picked her up, took her up to his bedroom and laid her on his bed.

"We can't do this, Dominic, I'm not what you want."

"You're everything I want and more, Lia, having you around in the penthouse drove me crazy not being able to touch you even more." He stripped and got on the bed with her.

"Just relax and feel. I will go slow, just say no and I will stop." He began touching, her body began to shake, the sensations were making her moan; he pushed his finger inside her and kept touching her until she screamed, and it went on and on. Suddenly, he gently entered her; it felt alien then he stopped and kissed her.

"One push and your virginity is gone, tell me, Lia, that you want this."

"I want you please, Dominic." He pushed and she grabbed his arms and was about to cry out, but he gently kissed her and then he moved and pulled out and gently pushed in; she held her breath.

"Breathe, Lia, relax, you're very tense. I'm going to touch you." And he did, his finger touched her clit and she began to shake; he began to move and the tension was building up and she moaned, and suddenly, she tightened around him, and he came inside her. Lia's body shook with the feeling she had;

115

he was still inside her, but he was touching her face, kissing her. Suddenly, he went small, and he got up and came back with a cloth; he gently cleaned her and sat her on the chair. He stripped the sheet off the bed; she could see the blood and shut her eyes. He bent down in front of her.

"Let's go to bed. I want you in my arms. I want to feel your body naked next to mine." They crawled under the cover and she was face to face with him; he closed his eyes and she laid for a while, but she was watching him. Lia got up and walked on to the veranda; she grabbed his shirt. She heard him yell so she ran back into the room and got on the bed, and he cuddled her. He was mumbling in his sleep, and she eventually closed her eyes. Dominic woke up; he was alone. Was he dreaming, did he have her in his bed? He drank almost a full glass of whisky but remembered how soft she was, how she came apart in his arms as he touched her, how he felt when he entered her; he wanted her again and again. Suddenly, the door opened and she came in wearing his shirt; she stopped and smiled. She came over, gave him a coffee and went over and sat in the chair sipping her tea.

"How are you feeling this morning?"

"I should be asking you, Lia."

"I'm fine, you need to put food in the kitchen cupboards, that's what they're for."

"I hardly stay here, unless I need to, then I order from my hotel."

"Figures, that's why no food." He throws her his phone.

"Order breakfast while I shower." She put the phone on the stall.

"I'm not hungry, I'm just saying." He goes to get up and looks at her.

"Come here, please." She shakes her head.

"I'm counting to three, and if you're not sitting on this bed, there will be consequences."

"Like what, Dominic? I'm not a child."

"You were where sex was concerned, cocky now that you're no longer a virgin." She puts her cup down and gets up; he thinks she is coming over, but she picks her clothes up and walks out.

"Guess you're asking for this, Lia." He opens the door, where the hell has she gone? He walks down the stairs and walks in the guest bedroom; she comes out of the bathroom and stops; he is stark naked. He grabs her and puts her over his shoulder and walks up the stairs to the master bedroom. He smacks her backside and she tries to get away. He throws her on the bed. Lia scrambles off.

"I'm going home, you're a bully."

"Bully, am I? We will see about that." He grabs her and he has her over his lap.

"Keep still, Lia."

"No, get your hands off me." He laughs.

"You wanted my hands on you last night, and against my better judgement, I did what you wanted, now it's my turn." He hit her with his hand, it took her breath away; he hit her again and she went still. Again and again, until Lia closed her eyes. Dominic stopped, and he sat her up. He tried to kiss her. She stood up, her feet wobbled, but she walked out the door. She sat on the glass step because it cooled her bottom. She went to get up and was suddenly in his arms; she went stiff.

"God, I'm sorry, Lia, forgive me." He laid her on his bed. She grabbed the pillow; she wanted to go; she wanted to stay; she felt a wreck. Suddenly, he was taking her pants down and

117

she started to cry. He had his hand on her bottom and was massaging her; the stinging stopped, and he pulled her into him. She closed her eyes and went to sleep; he laid cuddling her back. Lia opened her eyes; he was bending down and kissed her.

"I ordered breakfast. It's midday, you must be hungry." He pulled the covers back; he held a coat out to her and she put it on. He lifted her up, took her down to the kitchen. The small table was laid with everything you could wish for breakfast. She sat down and didn't flinch, the cream worked. She ate and he had a full English breakfast. Lia chose fruit and a cereal then bacon and egg and toast. She pinched one of his sausages, then she drank her tea. She got up; she needed a shower then she was going home. Lia turned to leave the kitchen.

"Stay with me today and tonight, I will take you home tomorrow afternoon."

"I can't, I need to go home, besides I have no clothes to change into." He gave her a small case and she recognised it.

"Where did that come from?" He looked at her.

"While you were asleep, I went to your apartment and got you some clothes."

"You went through my underwear drawers?"

"Yes, you need to demonstrate some of those in front of me, wow." She came up to him.

"How dare you, Dominic, you had no right to look through my things."

"You mean your sexy underwear?"

"I mean anything of mine." He grabbed her and kissed her.

"Go get dressed. I'm taking you out for the day." She showered, dressed and dried her hair. She came downstairs; he was on the phone.

"Thank you for your co-operation, you will be hearing from me." He looked up and smiled.

"Give me twenty minutes and we will be going, you look exquisite." She left the room, walked up to the library, walked in the envelope with the torn cheque in it was still there and her design book she stood looking out the window. He stood at the door.

"You know you should take the money, he wanted you to have it, Lia." She turned looked at him.

"No, never, if you want, give it to one of Russo's charities where it will do some good."

"Okay, if that's what you want, but take your book he wanted you to have it back." She looked at it but shook her head.

"Let's go before I change my mind, Dominic." She walked out the library; the book stayed where it was. He put his hand out and she took it. He helped her on with her jacket and they went downstairs to the garage. He helped her in the Aston Martin and he was driving; they headed for the motorway towards Paddock Wood, then they turned from the main road off the beaten track. A house came into view and he stopped the car.

He got her out and took her over to look down; it was like a small valley, beautiful to look at. The house was nestled in a dip in the ground.

"Does it belong to you, Dominic?"

"Not yet, I'm in negotiations to buy it. I thought as you're good at summing up property, you may be able to tell me if it's a good investment. I'm told it need a little TLC but it's sound and been empty for a year, the occupants went to Australia; the agent offered me a viewing; I have the keys."

"Why you Dominic."

"I like old buildings and this one is old, apparently." He put her in the car, and the nearer they got, the more excited Lia got. This was the type of house if she got married she would want to live in. They parked up and Dominic unlocked the door, and they walked in; it looked medieval, the exposed beams were beautiful; it was open plan just as Lia knew it would be. The wide staircase was mahogany and within keeping with the house. Sash cord windows were also within keeping with the property. The family had opened the downstairs up, but it needed pulling back some to make it cosy but within keeping with the age of the house.

"Well, what do you think, is it worth investing in?"

"Depends what they want for it, there is no woodworm, the house is sound, no damp as far as I can see, has anyone looked in the attic?"

"I have no idea, want to look?"

"Not really, but it's a nice house."

"They want two million for it, a bargain, yes, Lia?"

"A bargain, sure you pay more for a two-bedroom flat in Canary Wharf."

"Okay, I will buy it, but will you design the house for me then I can sell it on and make a profit. What do you say?"

"I can design the inside, put the lost features back, yes, I would love to play around with the house." They drove down, a country lane came to a pub where on the menu was a roast dinner. They went in and had roast chicken with all the trimmings, and apple tart and custard for dessert plus tea and coffee; they then drove back to the penthouse and Lia took her shoes off as soon as she got in. She went to make hot drinks when Dominic came out with two glasses of wine; he gave her one.

"A toast to us investing in a house for profit." She sipped the wine; it was delicious. She sat down with the glass.

"Would you like to watch a film or are you hungry?"

"Not really hungry, but some nibbles would go a treat with the film." He got on the phone and a waiter appeared with a tray of nibbles.

"If I'm staying again, we need to go shopping, this is stupid." They settled down with nibbles and wine in the cinema room. Lia chose *Pretty Woman* and Dominic smiled. Lia was on the floor on her belly, intent on watching the film. She had three glasses of wine and two pots of nibbles. Dominic changed into his sleep suit and he joined her on the floor amongst the pillows. She was popping cashews nuts in her mouth; they were her favourite with the sultanas. He gave her the nightdress off the bed. She sat up, undressed and slipped the nightdress on. The film finished and she went to get up.

"So lie on your tummy for me please, Lia." She did as he asked and he removed her pants. "Relax, I'm not going to hurt you." He got behind her and tucked a pillow under her tummy and suddenly he was in; he slipped his hand under and he was touching her, and she began to pant; he bent her legs and got so far into her she began to moan; he stopped and turned her over and took her all the way. He picked her up, took her up to bed and made love to her gently. She lay in his arms asleep; she was going to design the house he wanted to live in with

121

Lia after they were married, now he had a plan. Scheming was one thing Dominic Delgado was good at.

The weekend was over, and after lunch in the hotel, he took her back to her apartment; she shuddered when she walked in; she was not going there. She trusted Dominic, Mark was never coming back ever, but what he meant by that she had no idea. Dominic stopped for coffee then he kissed her and left, promising to phone her when he got back. Lia put the washing machine on, both dresses could be washed and hung up to dry. She made herself tea. There was a knock on the door, she was surprised it was Tony. She let him in.

"Where have you been, Lia? Your phone has been off." She looked, her phone was turned off, not her doing.

"Sorry, was it important?"

"Mark is back; he drew a blank in America, he wanted back in with me. When I told him I work for you, he got so angry he said he was seeing you, apparently you have something he wants."

"Well, whatever it was, he never saw me. I have been away all weekend." Lia went and made coffee and tea.

"I have a commission, a Tudor house to re-design inside. I saw it the weekend, white walls wooden beams inside and out a huge mahogany staircase. The owners put in all open plan; it needs defining a bit, but I would love to get my teeth into it; the house is my ultimate dream; a house if I could afford it I would love to live in it and I get to design it."

"For whom, Lia, let me guess, Dominic Delgado, right?"

"How do you know, Tony?"

"Come on, you must have been blind not to see he fancied you; he watched you enough when you were in the penthouse.

Be careful, Lia, there is something about that man, he has a dark side."

"Tony, if he decides to buy the Tudor mansion, then I will re-design it for him, but it will be just business."

"Lia, be careful, if Mark comes sniffing around, let me know. I think he is desperate to get back into the business again."

"I will never work with him after what he did to me." The tears started again.

"I can never make it right." Tony hugged her.

"I'm sorry, I hope I haven't frightened you. I just wanted to warn you."

"Security will never let him up here, Tony, see you tomorrow and thanks for the warning." She let him out and she washed up; she was going to bed. Her phone rang and she picked up.

"So, you switched your phone on."

"Yes, Tony came to see me."

"What did he want, Lia?"

"To warn me Mark was around. Apparently, he told Tony he drew a blank in America and wanted back in with Tony, but when he told him he was working with me, he got angry. He said I had something Mark wanted. I changed the subject."

"Look, get some sleep, there is nothing to worry about, trust me." The next morning, Lia took the four students with her to Canary Wharf; they were meeting the surveyors too because it was two flats into one. Lia had two girls in each flat taking measurements and Lia was liaising with the surveyors; she submitted the drawings she wanted to use to infuse the two flats into one; the only difference was extending the entrance to the apartment that they could accommodate. They took Lia's plans and said they would get back to her about the door. Lisa and Jenny came back with all the internal measurements from flat one and Lisa and Wendy flat two. They went back to the office. Tony came up to her.

"Dominic Delgado came in, he wanted to see you." The girls went for lunch and Lia to her office.

"Did he say what he wanted, Tony?"

"No, he said he would phone you and left. Nice car though, does he think he's James Bond, the Aston Martin must have cost a fortune."

"It's not like you to be jealous, Tony, watch your mouth." She walk around the table and watched him leave her office. Lia was sitting pencilling in the colours she wanted on the walls when Tony walked in and sat down.

"Look, I was out of order, I'm sorry." She put her pencil down.

"It's not like you, Tony. I'm sorry things turned out the way they did. Why do you still want to work in this business, you can do anything you want, tell me how much did you leave with." She looked at him.

"Ten million, Lia." She was shocked that was what would have been left over from the last build.

"Where did the rest go to, Tony?"

"Mark was in deep gambling, Lia, the business was about to fold; it was you who kept it afloat, the last building you designed gave him money to pay his creditors. I transferred the money into another account and he left with five million, fled to America. I think they caught up with him, Lia, he seems to have disappeared."

"What makes you think something has happened to him?"

"Look, we were partners for ten years before you came aboard, as bad as he got gambling, it was what he did to you made me wash my hands off him, but it's hard not to want to see he is okay, but there is nothing, no sign of him."

"Like all bad pennies, he will turn up at some time, Tony." She made him a coffee, but Lia was now worried. Her phone went, it was Dominic.

"I came by, you were out, everything okay?"

"Canary Wharf with the surveyors, two actually, I took the students, they agreed with what I wanted, made a few alterations and said they would get back to me; it's a waiting game now; the girls did all the measuring up I wanted and now I'm in the planning stage."

"You can't plan till you get the go ahead, Lia."

"Yes, I can. I'm planning the colour scheme, the furniture I need, where I'm sourcing it from; there is a lot to do."

"Spend the day with me tomorrow, stay the night. I want to take you back to the house, take your advice."

"So you bought it?"

"Yes, I have just handed two million pounds over to the bank to wire to the owners. The house is mine."

"Congratulations, I will see you tonight."

"Can't wait, I'm going shopping." She smiled. Lia got on with her design. Tonight, she wanted answers, she was actually frightened to ask. She hated Mark, but she did not want him dead, or did she?

Lia drove to the apartments and parked in the garage. George was on duty and she gave him his cakes he liked, and he kissed her hand. She went up in the lift; she had a hold-all with her as she was staying; she needed answers. Was Tony right, did he have a dark side to him? He was Italian. The lift opened and he was standing there; he took her hold-all and she walked into the lounge. She took her coat off and he just looked; the dress was exquisite it clung to her body. Lia sat down.

"Would you like a drink, Lia?"

"Tea please."

"Not a glass of wine."

"No, thank you, Dominic, I drove my car here." She got up and went into the kitchen; he followed her in. She was making tea while he went near the fridge and poured himself out a glass of wine. She sat at the breakfast bar.

"Is everything okay, Lia?"

"I want to know what happened to Mark. Tony has been trying to get in touch with him." She can see he is angry.

"Mark is gone; he threatened you and you're asking me where he is? I don't believe you, Lia, remember when I came to your apartment and he was going for you and I had him in an armlock? He would have hurt you yet you're concerned about him." She walked back into the lounge. He turned and looked at her.

"So tell me, Lia, what do you think I did to him, because I wanted to kill him and I could easily have broken his neck but my security took him away."

"So where is he, tell me."

"So you can tell Tony, did you tell Tony he was in your apartment?"

"No, I said I had not seen him and he couldn't get to my apartment because of the security."

"You said that to Tony because you knew I had taken care of Mark and he would never hurt you."

"So just tell me if he is safe." He turned and looked at her.

"You think I had him killed? I wanted to, but I'm not that person you think I am. He is working in Monte Carlo. I have a fleet of yachts, he is learning to crew on one of my yachts." He handed her coat to her and walked out of the lounge. Lia picked her hold-all up and went towards the lift; she pressed the button.

"You're never to come here again. Goodbye, Lia, have a nice life." She entered the lift, got in her car and drove away. She finished the apartment in Canary Wharf; it took six months, two months to get the go ahead. She missed him, but as the months went on, she tucked the hurt behind a wall she built; she kept busy and her business with Tony's help went from strength to strength. Her mum was worried about her, she was running herself into the ground. Nancy came to see her. There was a knock on her door and she opened the door to Nancy. Lia smiled and hugged her.

"I'm up doing some shopping. I thought I would come see you." Lia took her in the kitchen.

"Tea, coffee? I have one of those coffee machines, care to try a cappuccino?" Nancy sat down.

"I would love one." Lia made her one and she gave her a cinnamon bun.

"This is delicious, Lia, I need to get some."

"I made them; cooking relaxes me. So what were you shopping for?"

"That's what I came for, we're going to Italy for three weeks. Your mum was hoping we could get you to ease up and come."

"Where are you going in Italy?"

"Mr Delgado asked us if we would like to go back to the chateau and Donna wanted you to come."

"No, Nancy, it's the last place I would go, besides the invitation was not aimed at me; it never would be."

"Why, Lia, tell me, I would never tell your mum. Something happened, we both know it did. You're running yourself into the ground, come have a holiday with us; the chateau is huge, you can get lost in the place."

"I have no idea. I never ever stepped inside."

"But you designed the infinity pool, how?"

"From here, Nancy. I never ever saw it, only in pictures." Nancy stayed an hour and left. Lia sat and cried; she tried not to because crying just made her breathless. She sat, drank tea and put the colours into the latest apartment she was designing. She didn't want to think of where her mum and Nancy were going, it meant he kept in touch with them. October in Italy was still warm, but here in England, the winter was beginning to show itself. The security rang up.

"Miss Westlake, a Mr Delgado is in reception, he wants to come up; he is not on your guest list."

"Let him up, I will see him." He knocked, she opened the door, turned her back and he followed her in. She stood in the lounge near the couch; she never sat down. He looked at her and smiled.

"Why are you here, Mr Delgado, you have five minutes then I want you to leave." She was now telling him what he said to her months ago; she could be just as assertive.

"So, I'm not going to be offered a coffee, Lia? I have something I need to give you." He handed her over her design book.

"It's no use to me and it belongs to you. I'm selling the apartments and the penthouse and running my business from Italy. England has no interest to me anymore. You need to take it or it goes out with all the trash not needed." She looked up at him, he could see by her face he had hurt her and he hated that; he felt he needed still to hurt her. He also handed her a set of photos.

"Just to prove I'm not a murderer, pictures of Mark; he came good and is happy working the yachts, and he gave me a letter for you. I think it's an apology for what he did."

"I never said you were a murderer, Mr Delgado, but you said yourself you could have broken his neck. I just needed to know because your security took him, not you, but you never gave me time to finish the sentence. Please I need you to go, and yes, I will keep my design book, add it to the rest I have." She sat down. He walked to the door. She never looked up but heard the door close. Lia ran in the bathroom and was sick. Lia got to the office Monday morning, she had to see Judy as she needed pillows for the apartment to add the finishing touches. She got to her shop, and when she was walking to Judy's office, everything went black. Lia opened her eyes, she was in a cubicle. Judy was sitting beside her. She stood up, pressed a button, the curtain opened and a man in a white coat walked in.

"Welcome back, we were beginning to worry, Miss Westlake."

"Where am I, Judy?"

"You fainted in my shop. I sent for an ambulance, we could not wake you up; you scared me, Lia."

"Sorry, I have not been sleeping very well the last few days."

"Your blood pressure is high, your pulse rate is erratic, if sleeping is the problem, then I'm a Dutchmen's uncle," said the doctor looking at her intently.

129

"You are working too hard, you need to slow down or you're liable to have a stroke. You're what, twenty-nine? Give yourself a break, Miss Westlake, life is not all about working, slow down, fainting like you did means your body is telling you need rest, and I mean rest for at least a month. I will be back in an hour, so rest."

"Lia, you went out like a light. Tom caught you or you would have hit your head; you scared me. I phoned your mum, she is in Italy on holiday, if only you had gone with her, you need some quiet time." Judy could see tears; she held her hands.

"Tell me, Lia, maybe I can help."

"I need to focus, if I cry, I have difficulty breathing."

"You need to tell the doctor, Lia, maybe you need to stay here." Her phone rang and she answered.

"Mum, I'm fine. I fainted and Judy called an ambulance. I'm in the casualty ward, but the doctor is coming back to examine me in an hour. Stay in Italy, it's a false alarm. I will phone you in a few days, promise." She laid down, closed her eyes; now Judy is worried. She heard voices, and suddenly, she saw him: Dominic Delgado talking to the doctor. He called Judy out from behind the curtain.

"Take her key, Judy, and pack her a case or two for a month. I'm taking her with me, including her music and anything else she will need. The chauffeur will take you and bring you back here, meantime I need to talk to Tony." He walked off and Judy went with the chauffeur. She packed two cases, more than she would actually need; it gave Lia a choice. Her music iPod and her iPad, the charger, she was hoping she never forgot anything. The chauffeur took the cases, and Judy locked the apartment up making sure nothing was left on except the electric, the fridge was full of food. Judy looked, she was not eating much. They got back to the hospital; she was still asleep. Dominic was sitting in the corridor.

"So what's happening? Lia is still asleep."

"I spoke to the doctor after he spoke to Lia's mum; she need complete rest so I'm taking her somewhere so she gets the rest she needs."

"You are the last person Lia needs to be around. I think all this stress she is under stems from you, sorry just my opinion."

"You're right, but she will be with my housekeeper and Mary and Lia will get on fine. I won't be around. I want her well and rested. I promised her mum I would make this right. I'm doing my best." The doctor came along and he gave Dominic the tablet from the pharmacy.

"One twice a day after food for two weeks. I call it the wonder drug, it makes you hungry and helps you relax, just what the doctor ordered. Miss Westlake is all yours."

"If only it was that simple, doctor." They walked back into the ward. Lia was drinking tea.

"Lia, look you're not fit to work, so go with what Dominic is suggesting."

"Your mum is beside herself worrying so I assured her I would take care of you, so you have a month's rest, no work; hard I know but essential. I have a course of medication you have to take twice a day after food for two weeks. We need to get going. We are dropping Judy off and she will be down to see you. Tony is organising everything while you're away." Lia thanks the doctor.

"You have to re-charge your batteries now and again; you have been running on empty for weeks now." She gets in the car with Judy.

"Can you deal with the pillows in the sky view apartment, then it's done, please, Judy, I owe you one."

"If it will stop you worrying, then yes." Judy got out, kissed her and they drove off. Dominic got in the back. She sat as far away as she could ignoring him, looking out the window.

"Rest for a while." He tilted the seat and covered her up; she was fast asleep. How would she react when she saw the house Dominic had no idea; he was dropping her off and leaving going to Italy; he had business he had to deal with. It took an hour and the house came into view; she was still asleep when they drew up. Mary opened the door. Dominic carried her in; he was shocked at how light she was. He laid her on the couch and covered her up. They walked to the front door. Maurice carried the cases up to the bedroom.

"Mary, she needs rest and food, God, she is like a feather, feed her please, these tablets have to be taken twice a day after food. If you're worried, phone Arthur Miller, he will come and see her. You can ring me on this number, but I'm going to Italy for a week. I have urgent business." He kissed Mary on the cheek and was gone. Mary unpacked the cases and brought her books and her music iPod, her iPad downstairs and left them where she could see them. Lia slept for two hours, then suddenly she woke up. This was not the hospital, this was the house she first saw with Dominic. She sat up she needed a wee and knew exactly where to go. This was weird like a dream except it was not a dream; she could smell food and she was hungry. Lia walked out into the kitchen and Mary was busy cooking; she looked up and stopped what she was doing.

"I'm sorry, did I startle you? My name's Lia."

"Mary, I'm the housekeeper. How are you feeling? You have been asleep for two hours." Lia stretched her shoulders.

"I needed the sleep, Mary, how did I get here? I was in the casualty ward at St Stephen's Hospital."

"I don't know any of that Dominic with Maurice brought you here."

"Where is he, Mary?"

"Gone, ma'am, to Italy. He has urgent business; he said he will be back in two weeks."

"Two weeks? He expects me to stay for two weeks?"

"No, ma'am, he told me a month." She sat down. Mary gave her tea and some toast, she ate and drank the tea.

"So when was the house finished?"

"Reg and I moved in three weeks ago; we live in the small cottage in the grounds; my Reg is the gardener. The house is extensive, would you like me to show you where everything is?"

"No, Mary, I know where everything is unless he diverted from my design."

"Your design, you designed this house? It's beautiful; you are very clever."

"Not clever enough. I was shown this house a long time ago. Mr Delgado asked me if I thought it was worth buying and I told him yes. I sat at work daydreaming about designing the inside of this house and this is what I came up with." Mary was shocked this young woman was the one he spoke about with affection but also with such sadness.

"So Mr Delgado used your ideas?"

"Seems like it. I was told this was being sold."

"No, Mr Delgado said he was going to live here." He started the inside of the house six months ago.

"Miss Lambert was in charge; she had a team of twelve helping. He came down often to see she stuck with the design, all except the master suite that was a bone of tension, but it sorted itself out. They argued, he took her to dinner, the next day harmony again. When it was finished, he took her back with him to London; he seemed fond of her.

"Reg and I stayed in the hotel, the cottage was the last to be made livable, but Reg did the garden while the house was being renovated; they investigated how the garden should look and the gardeners were brought in; they found an overgrown orchard as well as other things. Reg thinks the last owners just concentrated on the house, not the surrounding ground.

"We need some dinner, Reg will be in soon. I was going to make a meat pie with cream potatoes and vegetables, sound good to you, Lia?"

"That would be lovely, Mary, thank you. I'm going to find my book, I hope Judy my friend packed it for me."

"So you have no idea where the library is, follow me." Mary took her through the smaller lounge then through a door and the library from the penthouse was there.

"Enjoy, I will bring you a drink as soon as I have the pie in the oven." Mary shut the door. Lia sat down; she had tears, but she brushed them away; she needed to get strong then she was leaving. Lia picked it up, *Pride and Prejudice*, appropriate she thought. Mary came in the door, Lia was asleep with the book on her lap so she woke her up.

"Tea, Lia, dinner in an hour. I see the book was boring."

"No, Mary, it's my favourite bedroom read, just tired that's all." Mary left her and went back to the kitchen. Reg came in.

"How is the patient, Mary?"

"She is nice, no trouble at all. You know, Reg, I reckon she is about twenty-six, but something has happened to her, what it is, I have no idea, but at the moment, she needs a lot of rest." Lia came into the kitchen and sat at the table. Mary dished her up homemade meat pie, creamy potatoes and cauliflower and runner beans. Lia was hungry and she ate well but refused dessert; she had a glass of iced water and took her pill, and then she went back into the lounge.

"Thank you for dinner, Mary. I'm going up, see you in the morning." She took a bottle of water with her. Lia decided to shower. She dried her hair, pinned it up and went to bed; she closed her eyes and she was gone. Mary's phone went, she knew who it was: Mr Delgado, the call came from Italy.

"How is she, Mary?"

"You mean Miss Lia? Fine, she had been reading then she had dinner now she has retired for the night. Sir, tell me why did I not need to show her around, she knew this house better than me, strange seeing she had never seen inside the house till today."

"Mary, I will be down at the end of the week when Lia I hope will have gained some of her strength, please do not tell her I'm coming."

"Very well, sir." Under Mary's care, Lia began to build up her strength and she could finally eat a meal without feeling sick. The tablets helped, they made her relax, but taking anti-depressants was not the way to go, so after a few days, Lia stopped taking them. Four days in, a doctor came to see Lia, her name was Doctor Jules; she walked in the lounge while Lia was reading.

"Good morning, Miss Westlake, my name's Doctor Jules. I hope I'm not disturbing you, but the hospital put you on my books why you are here." She sat down and Lia sat up.

"So, how are you doing, you seem very relaxed, may I take your blood pressure?" Doctor Jules took her blood pressure and her pulse; she seemed to Lucy to be totally relaxed.

"So far so good. I need to weigh you, do you know you have lost almost a stone in weight, you left the hospital at seven stones." Mary brought in some scales.

"If she hasn't put on weight, I'm doing something wrong because her appetite has got a lot better since Monday." Seven stones and four pounds, she was improving.

"The rest is doing you good." Mary brought in tea for both.

"Tell me, Lia, you're twenty-seven, why did this happen? Pressure from work, not enough sleep, a relationship that's gone wrong, not taking time for yourself?"

"I spent eight weeks driving around Europe being a tourist, my life took a nose dive when I came back and decided to start my own business, and it was fine then things happened and I made a wrong decision and I lost it. I need a way out, crying would have helped, but I couldn't because if I started crying, my breathing got laboured. So I held it all in so much my tummy started to rebel and then food became a problem and I fainted, ended up in hospital, and now I'm here for a month. I'm not stupid, I now know what I have to do, and when I get back to full health, trust me, this will never happen again. By the way, I'm almost twenty nine."

"So, you're relaxed so the problem has righted itself?"

"No, I just have to find a way to live with it instead of pushing it to the back of my mind."

"Lia, I'm not only a doctor I'm a stress therapist so if you want to share, I'm sure I could help, and it's confidential you are my patient while you are here."

"Tell me, Doctor Jules, who is paying your fee, Dominic Delgado?" From the look on her face, the answer was yes. Lia got up.

"If you'll excuse me, I need some fresh air." Lia walked out the room. Instead of crying, she was angry. She phoned Judy.

"Hi, honey, how are you? I was going to phone you, but I was told to give you a week."

"A Doctor Jules just did a visit. I have put on four pounds. At this rate, in a month I will be fat." Judy laughed.

"So where are you, Lia, I will come see you."

"A Tudor mansion in darkest Kent. Dominic brought me here once for advice on buying the mansion; we were talking then, well, more than talking, it was empty, it belonged to a couple who moved to Australia, two million they wanted for it. I remember telling him an apartment in Canary Wharf went for more than that. I'm sitting in the library, the one that was in the penthouse; it's beautiful, now the walls are up, the colours are vibrant and the furniture I think a lot came from the penthouse."

"So how long are you staying, Lia?"

"As long as Dominic stays away, for at least another week, may be longer. I have put on four pounds, Judy, I never realised how thin I had got. Mary his housekeeper is a darling;

she looks after me so well and her cooking is a dream, nothing fancy, just wholesome food, and I love it."

"Okay, give me till the weekend, I will find out where you are and surprise you." Lia decided to put her jacket on to walk in the garden. Mary was watching her, she was smiling as Lia looked tons better. Her phone went.

"Mary, you're doing a grand job. Doctor Jules tells me she has gained four pounds thanks to your cooking. Look, I'm not coming down, Lia need no stress, please keep doing what you're doing. I'm very grateful you have no idea how much." Mary put the phone down. Domino Delgado is in love with her patient.

"Well, I never." Reg came in the kitchen.

"Surprised to see me, Mary? I came in for my coffee and piece of cake."

"No, sorry, Reg, I just realised something, that's all." Lia walked down to the orchard, there were twenty trees as far as she could see; some still had apples on them. The begonias were still blooming, but soon they would die as the frost got them; the winter pansies were in bloom; she smiled, all different colours but each flower had a face on it. Lia would not be here when the snowdrop tulips and daffodils began to show their heads through the earth. Then comes the bluebells, the spring would turn into summer. She closed her eyes; she hated Mark she always would, but she knew Dominic would not have killed him, but his security guys would have and now he had a second chance working in Monte Carlo, good luck to him. Suddenly, her phone rang she sat on the bench, she look her mum she was still in Italy she was guessing the chateau.

"Mum, how are you?"

"More to the point is, how are you, Lia?"

"I'm fine, I'm taking it easy."

"Dominic said you are staying at the mansion and his housekeeper is looking after you, Mary I think he said."

"Yes, I'm okay, how are you enjoying yourself, and Nancy?"

"Darling, we're staying another two weeks; it's beautiful here. When you're better, you need to come out, it's very relaxing, but it's a relief to hear that you are being looked after by Dominic's housekeeper. I must write and thank her."

"Mum, I'm in prison for a month, three weeks to go tomorrow. I'm not doing anything, just doing what the doctor ordered: resting, reading and at the moment, by the orchard admiring the view. See you when you get home, we will have dinner. I love you."

"Lia, I love you, darling, bye for now."

"How is she, Donna?"

"She sounds better, Nancy. Dominic told me she is gaining weight, a good sign. Where did this all go wrong?"

"Dominic Delgado, that's where. Donna, don't hold your breath, they will never be a couple." Judy phoned Dominic and he had her picked up on Saturday afternoon and deposited at the mansion. Mary let her in and Judy introduced herself. Lia was in the lounge. Mary would get a tray. The door opened and Lia looked up, she was shocked; they hugged and Judy was pleased to see she looked tons better. Mary brought in a tray with tea, coffee and a homemade cake.

"Lia, we have put your friend in the bedroom by yours if that's okay."

"Thank you, Mary, that's fine, and as there is two of us, we can help, just say the word."

"Get away with you, I'm cooking a chicken and making a salad and salute potatoes, ready in two hours, so eat your cake." She left the room. They ate the fruit cake and drank the hot drinks.

"So was this mansion like this when you came with Dominic to see it?"

"No, this is all my design."

"Your design, Lia, how come?"

"This Tudor mansion was my dream. After we left, I started drawing, not upstairs but here on the ground floor. I knew exactly what I would have done with this house; the walls that needed re-instating to bring it in and make it cosy but fitting in with the original house; the people who live here made it open plan. I designed all this, Judy, and somehow Dominic got hold of my design, how, I have no idea but used my ideas to make it a home."

"Have you asked him why, Lia?"

"No, when I woke up, I was on the couch and he was gone, he left me with Mary a week ago."

"So this ground floor is you and upstairs is what?"

"Lovely but very modern; it's beautiful, you'll see two floors of guests bedrooms and at the top the master suite."

"Can we?"

"No, don't ask, the top floor is locked, Judy, and I'm not interested, trust me, nor would you be either."

"I would if I was single like you, but I'm seeing someone, just casually."

"Who, you have to tell me at least I will have something to smile about."

"Look, if you really feel uncomfortable staying here, come home with me, I promise I will look after you, make you rest."

"No, I'm staying, Judy, for the next three weeks I need to." Dominic got the low down on the weekend, and when Judy left Sunday evening, Lia was fine, Mary said the best she had been. The doctor came the following Friday and she was weighed; she put on three more pounds, she was seven stones and seven pounds; she was walking a lot, her blood pressure was stable and no stress. Doctor Jules tried to get Lia to talk to her, but the subject was personal and she was not sharing. Lia was getting restless, and on Thursday, she phoned Tony to see how things were going.

"Lia, how are you doing?"

"Fine, Tony, any new clients yet?"

"Well, the girls finally finished dressing the three apartments with Judy last week on Tuesday and we have signed them off; we have an apartment in Knightsbridge, the clients requesting you, so it is on hold for three weeks and she is okay with that. There is another apartment in Canary Wharf, apparently the woman living in the penthouse has had a few neighbours in and one requested our services. I'm going along to measure up and take pictures."

"Okay, do that then send me through the pictures and the measurements, and I can work from here."

"You sure, Lia, you have another twelve days 'rest."

"Tony, I'm going up the wall, there is only so much sleeping, eating and reading I can do. I'm even counting the apples left on the trees in the orchard."

"Okay, I will send it all through tonight, welcome aboard."

"Thank you for looking after my business. I will do the same for you when you have a break down." She signed off, the door opened and Mary came in, she saw her smiling.

"You're looking happy."

"Mary, I'm going back to work."

"You're leaving, Lia?"

"No, not yet but soon, Mary, but when I'll leave, I'm going to miss you."

"Okay, so dinner in an hour, okay."

"Thank you, I'm starving." Mary went in the kitchen, she wanted to phone Dominic but should she? She finally decided she needed to, it was her job on the line. His secretary answered, he was on his way home. Twenty minutes later, her phone went.

"Mary, everything okay?"

"Sir, Lia said she is going back to work."

"So is she leaving, Mary?"

"That's the point, she was so excited, but she said not yet, so I'm not sure what's happening, but I thought I should inform you."

"I will be down in the morning, we never had this conversation, right?"

"Yes, sir, I will leave it to you." Lia came in for dinner. Mary put on the table roasted lamb, tiny baked potatoes, green vegetables and a sauce made of mint and rosemary. Lia ate quite a lot and helped clear away the dishes and the leftover food. Dessert was a fruit full with whipped cream, and Mary poured a glass of wine each. They cleared the kitchen up. Lia went back in the office, she was using the big table. Mary brought her in some tea; she had her earphone in and she looked up.

"One minute, Tony, thank you, Mary, I will close the office up when I'm finished, and thank you for a beautiful meal. Mary just brought me in tea." Mary left the office, whoever she was talking to she seemed happy.

"So she wants to lose one bedroom so she will have two bedrooms and the master bedroom, give me the measurements and send the photos, they will download and I will lay the measurements on paper, make a design book. I need to do it by hand, this will keep me from being bored." Lia finally went to bed, it was late; she locked the office, his office. The next morning after breakfast, Lia was in his office; she was busy measuring and was drawing; she never heard the door open, and suddenly, she sensed she was not alone. She looked up and he was leaning against the wall, smiling.

"So who gave you permission to use my office?" She put her sketch pen down.

"Who gave you the right to steal my designs?" He just looked, then walked towards the table.

"I knew it would not take you long to realise the downstairs of this house is you, Lia."

"You were given my design book you're no different to Mark, then all this is to get back at me in a way, right? Dominic, having me stay here a month means you can rub my nose in it, right?" He just looked at her.

"If you had not been so ill, I would've taken you over my lap and spank you till you begged me to stop." She just got up from the table, folded the paper up, picked up her iPad and walked out of the office. Mary saw her face and she was shocked.

Lia walked up the stairs and phoned Judy, all she said was, "Judy, please come and get me." Judy phoned Dominic.

"What the hell's going on? I just got a phone call from Lia, she wants me to come and get her."

"Then come and get her, Judy, I can't keep her here, maybe its best if she is as far away from me as possible. I'm losing my temper." It look Judy an hour and she knocked on the door. Reg opened the door.

"Where is she, Reg?"

"In her bedroom, packing. I think Mr Delgado is in his office, there were words." She knocked on the door, he opened the door and she walked in.

"What the hell is going on, Dominic? I left her last night, she was happy, she was designing an apartment in Canary Wharf. Tony was faxing over the measurements, she told me all this was her design."

"Take her home with you, Judy, she accused me of being like Mark, that I stole her designs."

"She told me she designed the bottom of this mansion and this is exactly as she had designed it. So technically, you did steal her ideas.

"So you need to tell her how and why."

"No, apparently, I kept her here so I could rub her nose in it."

"Well, to Lia that's exactly as she sees it." He went in his drawer and he came over to her and handed her a document, a set of deeds, the mansion belonged to Lia, he bought it in her name. Judy looked at him.

"You need to tell her, Dominic, having her ill again is not an option, according to Reg she is packing. I'm staying here, sort it out now." He walked up the stairs, walked along the corridor and pushed the door open; she was stuffing clothes in her cases; she looked up.

"Get out, I'm almost finished." He came up to her and she stood up, and suddenly, he picked her up.

"Let me go or so help me I will scream." He took her back up the corridor up the stairs then up another set of stairs and he unlocked a door. He walked in a short corridor and a door. He put her down, unlocked the door and made her walk in. The master suite, a lounge and double doors, she could see leading out to a veranda; she turned to open the door.

"Judy is in my office, we talk, then you can leave forever." She folded her arms and looked through the glass doors; she turned and looked at him.

"Who gave you my designs, Dominic?"

"I took them when I went looking for you, Lia, the sketches were in your office in your apartment. I recognised the house, and yes, I implemented your design, this is the house you love, admit it. When I brought you here, you said, I remember, this house needs pulling in to make it cosy. Admit it, this is what you said. You left all those months. I had purchased the house for you so I had Sonya implement your design to the letter, but she did the bedrooms, you never got that far and I needed it finished." She was still leaving.

"Lia, this house and our future is in your hands. I want you. I have always wanted you. I love you, and all the shit that has been going on in our lives, I don't care about, but I do care about you. I love you but even me saying that you don't believe me, so take this, do with it what you want. but think very carefully before you destroy what we could have; it's in your hands." He opened the door and walked into the bedroom. Lia opened the document, it was a deed, the house was in her name, he bought the house for her.

Lia opened the door and he came out of the bathroom; he had a towel around his waist and she just looked. He could see the tears, but he was not helping her, she had to make the decision herself.

"You bought this house in my name, why, Dominic?"

"Because I saw the way you looked when you first saw the mansion and your face when you looked inside, then you said buy it you would pay more than two million for an apartment in Canary Wharf. I can't turn the clock back and put right what Mark did, but I'm not him, Lia, and you saying that hurt."

"I'm sorry I was angry and hitting out."

"At someone who loves you so much, God, these last three weeks have been murder. I wanted to be with you, but all I did was stress you out, when all I want is you in my arms." She walked over to him and she put the deeds on the side and leaned up and kissed him.

"Careful, Lia, I have nothing on under this towel." She leaned in and the towel fell onto the floor; he picked her up and walked into the shower with her and the water was soaking her clothes. There was a pile of wet clothes on the floor of the shower and Dominic had her on his bed naked. He gently made love to her and she moaned her way through everything he did to her, suddenly, she remembered Judy and Dominic smiled; she left hours ago. He had her in his arms and he was not letting her go, God, these last few months had taken their toll on him and then Lia getting sick nearly drove him mental.

"I think we need to eat, supper is being laid in the lounge. Mary is smiling again, I assume her patient is not going home." He helped her on with his towelling robe and they came out; he sat her down and the aroma of the food made her hungry. He was sitting across from her; he looked serious.

"When you have finished drinking your tea, I want to show you something, Lia." She looked at him.

"No more surprises please, I have had as many surprises as I can handle."

"This is for me, and trust me, you're going to like it and it's essential what I'm about to show you." She got up and he walked her back into the bedroom but over to a door she never noticed before, although what he was doing to her body, she was not concentrating. He opened the door and switched the light on and she just stared. A nursery, and it was beautiful.

"I know I must be scaring you, but I'm hoping we can at least think about it in the future."

Six months and Dominic got Lia down the aisle. July and Judy were her bridesmaids, the wedding was held in a marquee on the lawn in the garden of the Tudor mansion, and to get rid of all skeletons forever, Lia agreed to go to the chateau for a week during their one-month honeymoon; she made her peace with the past, and it was there in the chateau with the infinity pool Lia was sure she fell pregnant. Thirty-eight weeks later, she gave birth to a little girl and she called her Roselyn Lia Delgado. Dominic was infatuated with her and the happiest he could ever be except next time could it possibly be a boy. He was keeping his fingers crossed, if it happened, Russo Dominic Delgado would be in this world making their lives complete. A few years later and Dominic gave Lia Russo's will to read and the letter he gave Dominic, and she had tears; it was then that Lia knew Russo realised that Lia never sold her designs of the infinity pool to him because on the bottom of the letter he had written that:

I'm trusting you, Dominic, to make sure Lia gets her design book back, the one thing I know to be true Lia never sells her designs, she implements them, but her design books are hers. I have been following her career and I know this to be true. The million pounds is me saying sorry, forgive me for what I know to be true.

Russo,

Dominic came up to her she was sobbing so loud,

"Lia, I'm sorry, darling, God, I never gave you Russo's will to make you cry." She looked at him shaking her head.

"He knew, Russo knew I never betrayed him, Dominic, we spoke so much about what I had designed and I told him how the design books were mine, I never gave them to anyone ever and that's what he was saying because I told him even if somebody offered me a million pounds, I would never sell my design books and his words were to give me my design book back and a million pounds because he knew it was true and he asked me to forgive him." Dominic had her in his arms, and gradually, she stopped crying and somehow she knew Russo knew the truth. That night, Dominic had her in bed in his arms and he knew from now onwards Lia could live with the fact that what Mark did Russo knew it was not her.

She visited the chateau and swam in the infinity pool with the children knowing he was somewhere watching her and she now had the right to be there.